The Red Stone of JUBBAH

The Red Stone of Jubbah

Donald Tyson

Trade Paperback Edition

Text © 2020 by Donald Tyson

Cover art & interior illustrations © 2020 by M. Wayne Miller

ISBN: 978-1-888993-49-3

Editor & Publisher, Joe Morey

Copy Editor & Interior design, F. J. Bergmann

Weird House Press
Central Point, OR 97502
www.weirdhousepress.com

List of Illustrations

... its spires and towers stretched into the sky.   16

... starlight reflected from black claws and bared fangs.   58

I screamed each time it was applied.   80

... countless sharp white teeth were revealed.   114

... the stone had begun to glow a dull red ...   142

They fought with their teeth and fingernails ...   158

Chapter 1

"I just wish you would think about the consequences before you accept commissions from the Caliph, that's all," Altrus grumbled. "He's only using you."

"As long as I serve Moawiya, he is content to leave the necromancers in Damascus alone. Remember his predecessor, Yazid, who persecuted my kind without mercy."

"But when you fail to serve him, Alhazred, what then?"

"Why do you grumble so?" I asked him with a smile.

He pouted like a child, which looked ridiculous on his bearded, battle-scarred face.

"I am weary of traveling. It takes me away from the alehouses, and from the women who dwell above them."

"Ah, now we come to the nut of your discontent. You have a woman."

"I have many women, and I miss them all."

"But one woman who interests you more than the others."

He hesitated before answering. "It may be so."

"That's what I thought. Soon we'll all be treated to the pitter-patter of a little Altrus running up and down my staircase."

"If I were to devote my attentions to this woman alone, naturally I would buy my own house."

"As you choose, but there are few enough residents in that barn of a house of mine as it is. You and your woman—and your child, if it came to that—would be welcome."

"Thank you."

"I like being on the road again," Martala said brightly, changing the subject.

Altrus let the reins of his camel fall and spread his arms.

"What road? Look around you, girl. All I see is desert."

"Look behind us. That is our road."

I glanced over my shoulder and saw our three camel tracks meandering into the distance between the sand dunes. I smiled at Martala and she grinned back. Truth to tell, I was as happy as she to be away from the stink and press of Damascus. At times I thought about selling my house in Scholar's Lane and becoming a wandering mage. It was an idle dream and I knew it. Damascus was where I belonged. Still, it was good to have reason to leave its walls, lest I find myself turning into a fat householder of the city.

You are too restless of spirit to grow fat, my love, said Sashi, the familiar spirit who shared my body. None of my thoughts were hidden from her.

Men change as they mature, I thought back. *They become settled and brood over their responsibilities.*

Not you, she said with assurance.

I saw her face float before me against the backdrop of blowing sand, the beautiful human face of a woman with the full red lips and almond eyes that she adopted when we made love. Her head was wrapped in a blue silk hejab, and silver coins hung from its hem over her forehead. It was not her true visage, which was that of a minor djinn of the desert, a species known in the language of ghouls as *chaklah'i* that were regarded by ghouls as vermin because they crept close to share the remnants of the feast, but I accepted the illusion gladly. After all, my true face was more monstrous than hers.

While I had dwelt in the palace of King Huban of Yemen, serving as his court poet, I had committed the indiscretion of deflowering his only daughter and getting her with child. For this single minor fault he cooked and fed me the foetus of the stillborn infant, cut off my nose, ears and genitals and made me eat those also, then slashed my cheeks, burned me with hot irons, and whipped me. The result was quite different from the handsome features and graceful body with which I had been born. I still retained my pale gray-green eyes and abnormally white skin (a legacy, it was said in my village, of my mother's indiscretion with a djinn of the desert), but the face I presented to the world was no more than a glamour of magic, to be put on at need like a mask so that those I met did not run from me screaming in horror.

As a consequence of my castration, I could not make love with mortal women, but the magic of Sashi allowed me to achieve a sexual pleasure with her that was more intense and more sublime than any physical coupling. What did I care that her true shape was that of a long-legged, hopping creature with a large, round head in which were set enormous black eyes, bat-like ears, and rows of needle-sharp teeth? At least her djinn's hands were graceful and feminine, and the illusion of a beautiful woman that she projected in my mind when we made love suited me well enough.

"What are you thinking about, Alhazred?" Martala asked.

"The rocking of the camel sends my mind into the past."

"That is a place I don't like to visit."

I understood her meaning. Martala has been born into a clan of Egyptian tomb robbers. When she was nine her drunken father raped her. She murdered him with a knife and fled to the Egyptian city of Bubastis, the city of cats, where she served the king of thieves of that city as a seer for five years. It cannot have been a pleasant service, because she eagerly exchanged it for my companionship when I passed through that city in my wanderings, before I settled at Damascus. We had been together for more than a year, and I had come almost to trust her. Complete trust I offered to no one.

"How did the latest horoscope you cast for the Caliph turn out?" Altrus asked.

"Not good. I fear Moawiya has only a brief time left on the throne."

"He is hated for his compassion toward the people, which the mullahs see as weakness," Martala put in.

"Is that what they say in the marketplace?"

"It is."

"He will be assassinated or forced to renounce his title, mark these words," Altrus said with assurance.

"I fear you are correct," I told him. "It's too bad, because I like the man."

"If you liked him less we would not be here," he grumbled.

"You are not bound to my service," I reminded him.

"You're wrong," he said. "I was crippled of body when I came to kill you. Instead of killing me, you used your necromantic arts to give me back the full use of my sword. For that, I will serve you as long as you have need of me."

"You were a most determined cripple," I told him, recalling our last sword battle. Even though broken in body, he had very nearly defeated me.

"It was my pride that drove me. I had taken a commission to assassinate you for what you did in Alexandria, and even when my body failed me, my will compelled me to seek to fulfill it."

"And all of it over the theft of a scroll," I said, shaking my head.

"A very valuable scroll," he reminded me.

The scroll was safely locked away in my house at Damascus, along with my other treasures. There was little chance that anything would be taken from the house while I was away. The thieves of Damascus were as bold as any in the world, but none was crazy enough to rob the house of a necromancer. Truth be told, I did not even need to lock my door.

"I hate camels," Altrus said.

"Every time we travel on the desert, you say the same thing," Martala told him.

"From the way your camel behaves toward you, the feeling is shared," I said. The camel Altrus rode had never ceased to try to bite him or stand on his foot since our journey began.

"The only mount for a soldier is a good Arabian horse," he muttered. "Be honest, Alhazred, you hate these beasts almost as much as I do."

"We could not cross the Nafud Desert without them. Hate or love is beside the point. They are as necessary to those who dwell on the sands as the air we breathe, or the water we drink."

I patted the full waterskin that hung on my saddle. The touch reassured me. We could not be far from our destination, but if by some chance I had lost my way among the ever-shifting dunes, it was good to know that we carried several days of excess water.

"I don't know how you can stand the heat in those tight-fitting Persian rags," he said.

"The sun seldom bothers me," I assured him with a smile.

During my stay in Yemen as Huban's court poet, I had developed a liking for Persian clothing, which I had been able to indulge thanks to the thriving trade between Persia and Yemen. For this errand I had chosen to wear a tunic of my own design that a tailor at Damascus had sewn up for me. The flamboyant cut of the sleeves and neck was my innovation, but the gathering up of the long hem of the tunic at the sides, so that it hung down in front and in back like an apron, was a traditional Persian style. It was of white cotton and modestly ornamented at the hem, neck and cuffs.

Over my legs I wore loose cotton pantaloons, and tall leather boots that came up in front almost to my knees. My sword hung at my left hip from an embroidered and beaded baldric slung over my right shoulder, while a matching embroidered belt at my waist supported my money purse, my ivory-hilted dagger with its curved blade, and the bleached white skull of a ghoul who had once been my closest friend.

As was my usual custom, I rode with my head uncovered. The Bedouins considered this madness, but in addition to my strange green eyes and unnaturally pale skin, the anonymous djinn that was my father had given me an uncommon tolerance for the rays of the sun. I habitually cut my hair short and shaved my chin in defiance of the prevailing fashions of the Caliphate, yet my scalp and face never burned.

My companions had chosen to wear more conventional white thawbs and loose headscarves. Beneath their long robes I had managed to persuade them to put on pantaloons and boots as a practical measure. We could not be sure when we might find ourselves riding horses, and they also offered protection against the biting insects and sharp stones of the desert.

Martala was dressed as a young man. She often traveled in male garb so that she could go anywhere I went without the complications of feminine modesty. When her long dark hair was coiled up under her kufiya and her breasts were bound to her chest, those who saw her took her for a gangling youth whose beard had not yet begun to sprout. Glancing across at her, I realized her disguise would not work for very much longer. She was changing from a girl into a young woman, with all a woman's attributes. She might be able to bind flat her breasts, but she could not bind in her hips.

Altrus never bothered to try to disguise himself. It would have been futile. The large red burn mark on his cheek made him instantly recognizable. No one who gazed upon his sword-scared face or met his piercing dark gaze could judge him anything other than a soldier or a mercenary. His notched straight sword and straight dagger hung at his hips on unadorned leather baldrics that crossed on his chest. A similar plain belt at his waist supported his purse.

Anyone who saw us would take me for a man of substance who was traveling on a business matter, accompanied by his scribe, or perhaps by his young nephew, and by a mercenary bodyguard. This suited my purposes. There was no need for a more elaborate disguise.

At length, we rode up to the crest of a high dune and reined our camels to a halt. On the other side of the dune a flat expanse of ground extended away in all directions for many miles. Far to the west I saw a range of low mountains with scattered patches of green vegetation at their bases. It was a dreamlike place. The great rolling dunes of the desert simply stopped and gave way to the rock-strewn plain, which formed a kind of shallow basin among the dunes that towered above it.

"Why has the sand stopped?" Martala asked.

"No one knows. Some men think those mountains to the west, the biggest of which they call Jabal Umm Sanman, block the prevailing winds and prevent the sand from accumulating."

"Is that the oasis of Jubbah at the base of the big mountain?" Altrus asked.

"I believe so. I have never traveled here."

He glanced back over his shoulder the way we had come, and his charcoal eyes narrowed. I looked in the same direction.

"What did you see?"

"Movement."

"It was probably a dust devil."

He nodded but did not look convinced. We rode down the other slope of the dune and into the sandless plain.

"This is the strangest place I have ever seen," Martala said. "Oh, look over there."

She spurred her camel toward a tiny spot of bright yellow. We followed more sedately, and I saw that it was a lone flower, growing on a long stem up from a crack in the dried mud.

"Rain must have fallen here not too many days past," I said.

"We are no longer in the desert," Altrus said. "Praise the gods."

"Jubbah is the only oasis of any significance in all the Nefud. There is a permanent town there, where the Bedouins stop every year to water and fatten their herds. It is on the caravan road to Ha'il, which lies some eighty or ninety Roman miles further south."

7

"This is where we find the thing we came for?"

"This is where we look for it," I corrected.

We rode westward across the plain toward the mountains. Lulled by the slow jog of my camel, my thoughts drifted back to my recent interview with the young Caliph, Moawiya, in his palace at Damascus.

Chapter 2

A royal servant ushered me into a room the unadorned walls of which were lined with shelves overflowing with books and scrolls. Moawiya sat at a table covered with open books. He wore only a long white nightshirt and slippers on his feet, and looked as though he had just risen from bed although the morning was well advanced. I saw a brass oil lamp burning on the table and realized that he had studied all night and into the morning without noticing dawn at the windows.

He raised his head and smiled at me. There were dark shadows under his eyes.

"Welcome, Alhazred. It is good to see you again."

I bowed. His handsome face looked haggard and his beard was disordered, as though he had scratched it absently with his fingernails. Strands of dark hair hung over his forehead.

"You have been deep in study," I said.

"I have indeed. Please, sit down."

I sat in a plain wooden chair with a padded leather seat that was on the other side of the table. He noticed the light streaming in through the carven screens on the windows and put his hand behind the brass oil lamp to blow out its flame. A column of smoke spiralled up from its wick.

"It has been too long since we talked last, my friend. Affairs of state are so tangled, it takes all of my waking hours to unravel them, and while I sleep they tangle themselves anew and I must begin all over again."

"I am at your service, as always."

"I hoped you would say that, for I have pressing need for your talents. I will not waste your day with light talk, but will come straight to the heart of the matter. One of my spies has reported to me disturbing information concerning the affairs of Marwan ibn al-Hakam."

The name was familiar.

"He is a member of the royal family, is he not? I vaguely remember hearing a rumor that he recently traveled from Medina to live in Damascus."

"That is correct, he is my blood relation. Marwan and I are both grandsons to Umayya. He was forced to leave Arabia when the political tide turned against him. He covets my throne and has come to Damascus to be closer to me so that he can work against me in the council chambers."

"Isn't he an old man? Maybe he just came to Damascus for refuge."

"So he pretends. Yes, he is old, but he wants the Caliphate for the sake of his son, so that his line can form a new dynasty."

"Do you wish me to assassinate him?"

Moawiya laughed out loud. It was some time before he could bring his mirth under control. He wiped tears from the corners of his eyes and grinned at me.

"As attractive as your proposal may be, no, I fear it would not be expedient at this time. I've summoned you here to propose that you undertake another task entirely."

"You have only to name it."

His face became more serious.

"What do you know about the black stone?"

"You mean the black stone that is set in the eastern corner of the Ka'bah at Mecca?"

"The very same."

I took a few moments to collect the fragments of memory that concerned the stone.

"It is said to have fallen from the heavens. I have never seen it, but I have been told it is about the size and shape of an ostrich egg. It is mounted within a massive setting of silver that resembles the sexual parts of a woman. Mohammed himself is reputed to have placed it there. Men who travel to Mecca on hajj adore the stone as if it were a god."

The Caliph shook his head in wonder.

"Were you to say those things to a mullah, I don't know if all my power could prevent you from being stoned to death in the marketplace. But between the two of us, what you say is accurate, if heretical. Yes, the black stone is adored. When Mohammed came to Mecca, he took all the idols of gods and goddesses out of the Ka'bah and had them destroyed, but for some reason he treated the black stone with respect and had it mounted where it could be seen and kissed. He called the stone the Right Hand of God."

"I'm not following the direction of your words. Do you want me to steal the black stone?"

Again he burst into peals of laughter that had in them an edge of hysteria. I realized he had been up all night without sleep and that his mind was under strain. I waited patiently for him to comport himself.

"What most people do not know is that the black stone had companions. When it fell, other stones fell with it. One was a stone of roughly equal size but blood-red in color. Another was white. The black stone found its way to Mecca. The white stone was worshipped at al-Abalat, but almost nothing is said about it by scholars and it has been lost beneath the sands of history. For a while a red stone was kept in the city of Ghaiman. The most reliable chronicles say it was not the true red stone, but a false stone set up by the citizens of Ghaiman in their place of worship so that their enemies would believe the city unconquerable. Of course it, too, is gone now."

"I perceive it is this red stone that interests you."

"If the black stone is the right hand of God, as stated by the Prophet, then does it not follow that the red stone must be his left hand, which is the hand of judgment?"

"Why not the white stone?"

"The left hand of judgement enforces the laws of Allah. It punishes wrongdoers. It must be red because it is stained with the blood of the guilty."

This reasoning made sense, insofar as the symbolism of the colors was concerned. I wondered what all this ancient lore of stones had to do with me.

"What you have told me is fascinating, yet these stones are mere relics of past ages. Why do you concern yourself with them?"

His eyes widened and seemed to brighten with a kind of fanatical fervor.

"Legend tells that the man who possesses the red stone will become invincible in battle, and will go on to conquer the world. It is said that Alexander the Great once possessed it, and that when he died of disease at Babylon the stone was carried west." He pointed to a parchment scroll on the table before him. The ink on it was so old, it had weathered and faded to a pale gray, but the words could still be read. "This parchment and one other that I keep locked away in my private library intimate that the black and the red stones are the very Urim and Thummim mentioned in the holy books of Moses."

"Do you believe there is any truth in these legends?"

"That is not important. What matters is that Marwan believes them."

"If this red stone has been lost, what practical application can the legend have?"

"That is why I called you here. One of my spies reports that Marwan has recently become obsessed with a rumor claiming that the true red stone was in the safekeeping of the Thamud, an ancient people who have since perished from the world. The legend further states that after the death of Alexander, they carried it from the land of Persia to the oasis of Jubbah in the midst of the Nafud Desert."

"I have never heard of the Thamud."

"They were a race of men who dug into the sides of mountains to make dwelling places. God was not happy with them and punished them for their disobedience, or so it is said in the Koran."

"You know that I am not a great reader of the Koran."

"No, I suppose not," he said, eyeing me askance. "Your reading would tend more to the secrets of the tomb and the sepulchre. Let me speak for you the passages where the Thamud are mentioned."

He rose from his chair and stretched his stiffened back with a pained expression, then took a beautifully bound black book down from one of his shelves and thumbed through its pages.

"This is Surah 7, ayat 73 to 74:

"*To the Thamud people We sent their brother Salih. He said, 'O my people! worship Allah: you have no other deity other than Him. There has come to you clear evidence from your lord. This is the she-camel of God sent to you as a Sign. So leave her to eat within God's land, and do not touch her with harm, lest there seize you a painful punishment.*

"*And remember when He made you successors after Aad and settled you in the land, and you take for yourselves palaces from its plains and carve from the mountains, homes. Then remember the favors of God and do not commit abuse on the earth, spreading corruption.*"

He turned a page and read from it.

"This is Surah 7, ayat 77 to 78:

"*So they hamstrung the she-camel, and were insolent toward the command of their lord and said, 'O Salih, bring us what you promise us, if you should be of the messengers.'*

"*So the earthquake seized them, and they became within their home corpses fallen prone.*"

I considered these verses for a time.

"So the Thamud perished at the hand of God."

"The Thamud are no more. But one of their chief dwelling places was Jubbah. It is said they made their houses in the mountains that border the oasis on the plain."

"Has Marwan gone to search for the red stone at Jubbah?"

"No, but my spy tells me he has sent agents to search there

on his behalf. My spy says they are led by a ruthless man who will commit any outrage to get what he wants."

"What is his name?"

He shook his head. "That information my spy could not obtain. He was killed trying to get it."

"Why not let them hunt for this stone? It is most likely the stone does not exist, and even were they to find it and bring it to Marwan, it is probably nothing more than a common piece of rock."

"You do not understand its importance," the young Caliph said with sudden passion. "The red stone is a symbol of conquest. To the people, such symbols can be more potent than magic spells or djinn. Why do you think we rulers live in palaces and deck ourselves with uncomfortable robes that are covered with pearls and jewels? Why do you think we sit on thrones and carry scepters? Because they are symbols of our authority. If Marwan gets the stone, he will circulate its legend in the marketplaces of all the cities of the Caliphate, and the people will believe it. You know how credulous they are."

"What do you wish from me?"

He replaced his Koran on the shelf and resumed his seat. His face looked haggard, and it was more than a sleepless night that had made it so. He was being eaten up by his constant worrying and by his conjectures of what might come to pass. He leaned forward and met my gaze across the table.

"Gather your companions and go to Jubbah. Find out if there is any truth to this legend of a red stone, and if there is, locate the stone and bring it to me."

"What of Marwan's agents?"

"If they get in your way, kill them. I must have that stone."

I emerged from the palace into the morning sunlight, thankful that my personal concerns did not include the running of an empire, but resolved to do all I could to fulfill Moawiya's wishes. This red stone probably had no existence outside the pages of legend, but the excuse to leave Damascus for a while was not unwelcome.

... its spires and towers stretched into the sky.

Chapter 3

We rode across the plain toward the oasis, which was nothing more than a green patch in the distance. The shimmering waves of heat rising from the ground created mirages. One of them gave the appearance of a great white citadel on top of Jabal Umm Sanman. By unvoiced common consent, we paused to admire it. The stones of its walls were enormous, and its spires and towers stretched into the sky.

"They say that mirages in the desert are more than just illusions," Altrus said quietly as he squinted at the citadel.

"What else do they say?" Martala asked.

"They say that sometimes, mirages are echoes from the distant past of things that once were but are no more."

"It may have been a dwelling of the Old Ones, before they created the race of men," I murmured.

"Who told you these Old Ones created us?" Martala demanded.

"Things that burrow deep beneath the ground and speak of the past in dead languages."

She could not tell if I were serious or only joking, but she held her tongue.

As we drew nearer to our destination the mirage vanished. I saw that the town of Jubbah was defended by walls of mud bricks. Houses had spilled outside the fortifications, which indicated a growing resident population that had little fear of attack from the desert. Bedouins were camped beside this wall, their goats and camels grazing sedately on the green grass that stretched for a considerable distance behind the town. On the opposite side of Jubbah was the encampment of a sizeable caravan.

"We seem to have arrived at a busy time of the year," I observed.

Through the open gate we rode into a kind of chaos of shouting voices and waving arms. Everyone was selling something, and they competed with each other to make the most noise. My mask of glamour was firmly in place. When the merchants and beggars looked at me, they saw a young man of uncommon fashion sense and pleasant countenance, with strange grey-green eyes and a face clean-shaven. I would probably have been swarmed by them, but when they looked at Altrus, they fell silent and dropped their gaze. The red sear mark on his cheek coupled with his many scars gave him an intimidating aspect. Martala had pulled the end of her kufiya over her face so that only her grey eyes were visible.

"This place has a well-worn look to it," Altrus said. "How long do you suppose it has been here?"

"No one knows how old it is, but some scholars claim it may be as old as Damascus," I told him.

"By 'some scholars' you mean...?"

"Harkanos."

Before leaving the city I had taken the trouble to find out what I could about Jubbah, the Thamud, and the red stone in the library of my next-door neighbor, a necromancer named Harkanos. He was universally recognized as the leader of the necromancers of Damascus and, with the possible exception of the ancient sage Abdul-Basir, as the most learned among us.

"Nothing is written with assurance about the red stone, other than that it fell from the sky at the same time and place as the black stone presently at Mecca," Harkanos told me when he passed me a selection of ancient scrolls. "It is said that he who possesses the red stone is invulnerable in battle. But you already know this. My personal belief is that the black stone expresses the virtues of the moon, and the red stone those of the sun."

"Do you think there is any truth to the legends that surround the red stone?"

He shrugged and smiled at his young daughter, who played with a cat beneath a table in his library. As usual, the girl was naked. She seldom wore clothing in the house. She was a fey child with a sweet disposition but a strange, distant look in her eyes, as though she could see things others could not see.

"Who can say? The legend of the red stone has been unchanged over many generations. Such persistence often indicates a seed of truth, although sometimes the truth is as small as a mustard seed."

"What do you make of the Caliph's view that the two stones may be the Urim and Thummim spoken about in the holy books of the Jews?"

"It is possible. These stones were lost by the Jews many centuries ago. The passage in the book called Exodus would seem to speak against such a conclusion, for it is said that the stones of the Jews were placed inside the breastplate of their high priest, where they were used for divination, perhaps to find the guilt or innocence of one who stood accused of a crime. But it may be that those stones in the breastplate were only tokens of the true Urim and Thummim. If so, it does give rise to a troubling conjecture."

He paused and gazed out his window at the walled garden behind his house, where a servant on a ladder was tending one of the fruit trees. I waited for him to speak.

"If the stones of the Jews were used to decide guilt or innocence, as some believe, then one of the stones represents mercy, which the mystics of the Jews call *chesed*, and the other severe justice or punishment, which they call *geburah*."

"Why is that troubling?"

"If the black stone at Mecca is the stone of *chesed*, or holy mercy, that would mean the lost red stone of Jubbah is the stone of *geburah*, or divine judgment. It is always dangerous to get near to an instrument through which is channelled the wrath of a god."

We conversed amiably for over an hour, until he had exhausted his store of knowledge concerning Jubbah and the lost tribe known as the Thamud.

"I will leave you to your own studies, Alhazred. But first, I may be able to ease your arrival at Jubbah with an introduction."

He sat at his desk and took pen and parchment and wrote a brief letter, then folded it and sealed it with red wax, using his carnelian seal ring.

"What's this?"

"When you get to Jubbah, go to the house of a man who calls himself Thalmus. He is a sage of deep study who has devoted much of his life to the lore of the oasis and the mountains that brood over it. Give him this letter. He owes me a debt and will do what lies within his power to assist you."

Remembering the words of Harkanos, I patted my tunic and felt the reassuring shape of his letter in its inner pocket.

I asked directions to the nearest inn from a water-seller with three teeth who chattered like a monkey; I had to bend from my saddle and strain my ears to hear his reply above the noise of the street. He gave me a silver cup of water that was attached to his ewer by a silver chain. The water was surprisingly good. I dropped a coin into the empty cup and passed it down to him.

We followed his directions, and arrived at a large caravansary of two levels with an enclosure behind it for camels. Martala and I went inside while Altrus remained with our weary beasts. The keeper was a lean little man with flecks of grey in his beard. He ran this way and that, trying to accommodate the demands of the well-dressed merchants from the caravan who were his guests, and it was some time before I could attract his notice. While I spoke to him, he stared at the ghoul's skull on my belt.

"You want a room?" he repeated as though I had just uttered something insane.

"Two rooms."

He laughed harshly and shook his head. "I haven't got so much as a shed. Every room is filled four times over. Men are sleeping on top of each other."

I opened the drawstring on my purse and drew out a handful of coins. "Perhaps a mistake was made when you promised some of those men rooms."

His face puckered into a frown.

"I never promise a man a bed unless I have it, and I never take back a bed from a man when I've promised it to him."

"Your business ethics are laudable, if inconvenient," I told him.

"It doesn't matter; we can sleep under the stars," Martala murmured behind me.

"Will you at least feed and water our camels if I leave them in your keeping?"

This he agreed to do, for a price that would have been outrageous under any other circumstances. I paid him without complaint.

We returned to Altrus, and lingered to ensure that our mounts were well-treated, then walked through the crowded streets until we came to an alehouse. It, too, was crowded, but we managed to get a table in the corner and sat around it, drinking our ale. I gazed around at the extremes of humanity. Everyone was here, from the lowest cut-purse and sneak thief to the richest merchant. A few of them were mercenaries, probably in the hire of the caravan. They met my gaze without dropping their eyes. I wonder if any of them were the agents of Marwan ibn al-Hakam.

"How are we to find anything in this madhouse?" Altrus asked.

"We need to talk to a local wise man named Thalmus, who will know all the lore of Jubbah and the hills."

Altrus snorted in derision.

"Why would a man of such learning choose to live so far from Damascus?" Martala asked.

"I know not, but there is usually a good reason."

Across the room a young man of prosperous appearance stared at us over his ale. He sat alone at a table, yet no other man or woman tried to sit beside him, which seemed odd given the crowded state of the alehouse. I feigned disinterest in his attention and leaned toward Altrus.

"That man in the corner—"

"He rode into Jubbah through the gate just ahead of us. I saw him following us in the street."

"Is he a thief?"

Altrus glanced across the room and shook his head imperceptibly.

"He doesn't have the look. Not hungry enough. He's a killer, though. I can see it in the way he wears his sword."

He pushed himself to his feet and walked directly over to the young man's table. Leaning his scarred knuckles on the table's surface, he spoke quietly. I could not hear what he said because of the noise in the room.

"What's he saying?" Martala demanded. Sometimes she reminded me of a small child.

The young man began to protest hotly, his eyes flashing with dark fire. I could hear his raised voice but not his words. He jumped up, threw the little table aside, and drew his sword.

"This will be interesting," I told the girl.

Altrus had his sword out at the same instant. Their blades clashed and the men who sat drinking around them scrambled to get out of the way. The music of steel against steel continued for almost a minute with furious haste. The young man was a skilled swordsman, but it was obvious to me that Altrus was playing with him as a man will play with an impetuous boy. At every moment I expected to see his sword point pierce the other's heart, but Altrus held back the killing strike.

The keeper of the house and two of his hired men finally found the courage to intervene. The fight was stayed, and the young man spat out a few well-chosen insults, then turned on his boot heel and left. The keeper continued to remonstrate with Altrus, but was ignored. Altrus returned to his seat with a satisfied expression.

"He denied following us, but I don't believe him. Whoever taught him the sword taught well. He could kill most of the men in this room."

"But not you," I said with a smile, which he returned.

"No, not me."

"I'm glad you didn't kill him. We don't need the attention so soon after our arrival."

"Do you think Marwan's agent knows we are in Jubbah?" Martala asked me.

"That is the most obvious explanation for the man's behavior."

"Someone may have followed us from Damascus, and ridden on ahead to warn Marwan's agent of our coming. He probably set that young fool to watch us."

I remembered the movement Altrus had seen on the desert dunes, and realized that he was thinking the same thing. We had set a leisurely pace to spare our weary camels. It would have been an easy matter to follow us, and then on the last day of our journey ride past us behind the cover of the mountainous sand dunes.

When the serving girl came with her pitcher to refill our wooden tankards, I asked her if she knew of a sage named Thalmus who could tell us the history and legends of Jubbah. She had one of those chubby, round faces that seem to be perpetually smiling. She thought for a moment.

"There is a man of that name who lives alone in one of the big houses with walls around them at the back of town. He is said to be a scholar who came here years ago from Medina. But I don't know if he will talk to you. He seldom talks to anyone. For that matter, he seldom ventures outside his house."

I gave her a coin.

Chapter 4

We found the house without difficulty from the serving girl's description. The rear of the town was less crowded than the front, where the alehouses and vendors' carts were located, and the houses were larger, with walled gardens behind them that contained mature fruit-bearing trees. They were not grand houses by the standards of Damascus, but it was clear that this was where the wealthier residents of Jubbah lived. Everywhere there was greenness. The smell of the water close beneath the surface of the ground was so strong after our days upon the sands of the Nafud, it made me light-headed.

A manservant came to the wrought-iron gate when we pulled the cord of the brass bell that was mounted on a bracket near the top of the wall. He was a slender bald man of middle years who looked to me like an Egyptian. At any rate he wore a white linen skirt of Egyptian cut and an embroidered sleeveless vest that exposed his hairy chest. His movements were slow, his words were slow, and I have no doubt that his thoughts were slow as well. He listened with a doubtful expression, his black eyebrows almost touching, when I told him our purpose.

"We have traveled from Damascus to converse with your master."

"The master sees no one."

"We have a letter of introduction from your master's friend, Harkanos."

He extended his hand through the iron rails of the gate. "Give me the letter."

"No. I will put it into the hand of Thalmus."

He glanced down at Gor's skull on my belt, pondered a response, then went back into the house without speaking. At length he escorted us across the paved courtyard, through the entrance hall and into a room of modest size that I took to be the sage's study. There were many books on shelves, a globe of the world, an astrolabe, charts of the stars in the heavens, a small mummified crocodile that hung from the ceiling, glass retorts, and other instruments and objects that only a scholar or a mage would possess.

Thalmus was a frail man of around eighty years. He greeted us coolly, but after he read Harkanos' letter of introduction his manner warmed.

"How is my old friend Harkanos? It has been many years since we last talked together."

"He prospers," I said. "Since the death of Yazid, Damascus has become a safe haven for ... scholars."

He noticed my momentary hesitation and smiled.

"The studies of Harkanos are well known to me. He indicates in his letter that you are engaged in similar pursuits. Years ago I also had an interest in the arcane arts, which is how we came to meet."

"Do you still practice the arts?"

He frowned.

"No. I had an unfortunate experience that cured me of my curiosity. Come, all of you, follow me into my sitting room where we can talk in greater comfort."

The room was well furnished with a divan, a padded bench, and three armchairs, along with several low tables. The Egyptian servant brought us steaming reddish-brown liquid in tiny crystal glasses. Thalmus observed our dubious expressions as we sniffed our cups.

"It is a drink called tea. It is made by steeping dried leaves in hot water, and comes from the distant eastern land of Chin, where silk is made. Physicians say it is good for the digestion. I must confess, since moving to Jubbah, I've become quite addicted to it."

"We have it in Damascus," I assured him.

The rich aroma of the liquid filled my head. Even though my nose is missing, my sense of smell is as keen as it was in childhood. I sipped cautiously from my glass.

"Harkanos asks in his letter that I tell you all I know about the lore of the Thamud. He remembered me telling him in a letter that when I first came to live in Jubbah, I made a special study of them, for the subject fascinated me."

I set my glass down. The tea was quite bitter.

"If I may ask, why do you choose to live in so remote a place?"

A shadow of memory crossed his wrinkled features.

"That would be a long story and not one that I am prepared to tell at this time. Did Harkanos say nothing of the matter?"

"Not a word."

He nodded and seemed to relax.

"There are advantages to living on the oasis. The caravans that pass through here bring all manner of exotic goods from far-off lands, and keep us aware of the latest events transpiring in the greater world."

I glanced at Altrus, who met my gaze. We were thinking the same thought: the old man had come to the oasis to escape some fate or judgment. Whatever it might be, it was not a matter that pertained directly to our inquiry.

"In his letter, Harkanos writes that you wish to know about the red stone."

"We seek to learn its present location."

He studied my face for so long with his shrewd eyes, I wondered if he possessed the ability to see beneath my glamour of false appearance.

"You are agents for another, are you not?"

"That is a matter about which I am not prepared to speak," I said, echoing his own evasion.

"I understand. It was only a matter of time before the warring royal houses of the Caliphate turned their attention to the red stone, but I did not expect it to happen while I was alive."

"You knew men would come to search for the stone?"

"In the acquisition of political power, such symbols as the stone are invaluable weapons. Always when seizing power there is the need to justify its possession. The red stone would be a persuasive argument that its owner was chosen by Allah to rule."

"How did you know those seeking the stone would come here?" Martala asked.

"You speak forthrightly for so young a woman."

She looked at me, and I shrugged.

Drawing off her headscarf, she unpinned her hair and let it fall loose to her shoulders. "How did you know?"

He smiled at her. "I am an old man, but still a man. The day I cannot tell a woman's cheek is the day I wish to die."

"Will you answer my question?"

"Those seeking the stone will come here because there is nowhere else to go. In the lore of the red stone, all roads lead to Jubbah, and this is where they end. The legends say the stone was carried here, but they do not say that it was ever carried away."

"What of the stone that was once at Ghaiman?"

He made a dismissive gesture with his hand. "A fraud."

"Do you truly believe this red stone still exists?" Altrus asked.

The old man sat back in his chair to ponder the matter.

"That is a question I have asked myself daily since coming to dwell in this place, and each day I receive the same answer—perhaps. Perhaps the red stone exists. Or perhaps not."

We talked for some time about the Thamud and their connection with the red stone. Thalmus believed they had arisen as a people in Persia, or even further to the east, and had gradually worked their way westward over many generations, first inhabiting the southern portion of Arabia, and then moving north as the persecution against their religious beliefs increased.

"They are best remembered for their custom of carving their dwellings into the solid rock of the mountains and living in these charmingly decorated recesses, which more resembled Roman tombs than homes. It was not uncommon in those times for men to live in caves. We still have cave-dwellers on the shore of the Red Sea, you know."

"Did they bring the stone with them when they came to Arabia?" Martala asked.

"That seems most probable to me. Indeed, I think it likely that they brought all three stones, and that at some point in their custodianship the black stone was stolen and the white stone lost."

"It has always been a mystery to me why the Prophet, who destroyed every other idol and deity in the Ka'bah at Mecca, treated the black stone with such reverence," I said.

"I know not the reason, unless through his personal connection with Allah he recognized its holy nature."

"He probably knew the people of Mecca would not allow him to destroy the black stone, and decided to compromise. He let them keep the black stone in return for destroying the other idols in the Ka'bah," Martala suggested.

"That is a very cynical view, young woman," Thalmus said. "But you may be correct, at least in part. Of all the barbarous idols at Mecca, the black stone was the most revered."

"What of the red stone?" I asked, steering the conversation back to the topic that concerned me. "In your studies, did you find any historical reference to its worship at Jubbah?"

"I do not believe the stone was ever kept at Jubbah."

I held my features impassive, but my disappointment was keen. He must have perceived it, for he smiled slightly and raised his trembling hand.

"This oasis is only a watering place. The Thamud always made their homes in the mountains."

I glanced through the open window behind him, where the crest of the nearest mountain was visible between the waving fronds of the date palms.

"Are there Thamud dwellings on Jabal Umm Sanman?"

"I have not been able to locate any, and believe me, I have searched for them. You see the mountain? It does not loom so large against the sky when viewed from my window, yet it is some five Roman miles in length on its north-south axis, and twenty-five hundred cubits in height. There are great tumbled stones on its summit that resemble building stones, but their gigantic dimensions argue against this conclusion, and they are so ancient that no trace of the tools used to shape them remains on their surfaces."

"Maybe the Thamud dwelt on the summit of Jabal Umm Sanman, but their dwellings were destroyed by an earthquake, as it says in the Koran."

"No, these ruins atop the mountain, if indeed they are ruins, would be far older than any record of the Thamud that exists."

I thought of the mirage we had seen while approaching the oasis. The stones in the shimmering citadel had indeed been massive.

"What you will find atop the mountain," he said more slowly, "are carvings cut deep into the flat surfaces of the larger stones. I believe some of them were made by the Thamud and record a number of the sacred beliefs of that people, as well as the names of their gods."

This was encouraging information.

"Have you found any carvings that depict the red stone?"

"I believe so."

"Excellent. You must show us where they are."

"Unfortunately, that is not possible. My civic duties prevent me from leaving the town at present. A man has been arrested for murder, and I must prepare his appearance before the mayor and the town council for judgment. He is a poor, sick wretch who I fear will not live long enough to attend his own execution. However, I will describe where you can find the carvings."

Thalmus was an old man. It may be that he dreaded the prospect of climbing the rocks. I did not press the matter.

"Where are you staying in Jubbah?" he asked.

I related our unfortunate experience at the inn.

"I thought as much. With the caravan here, it was unlikely you would find a room for let inside the walls. You must do me the honor of staying in my house. Please, I insist upon it. I have empty rooms and you are in need of beds."

My protests were weak. Although I have often slept on the hard, bare rock beneath the stars, where one is available I always prefer a feather mattress.

"Good, that is settled," Thalmus said with satisfaction. "I will have my servants prepare you an evening meal and air your rooms. In the morning you can climb Jabal Umm Sanman and study the rock carvings for yourselves. Perhaps your young minds can make sense of a puzzle that has defeated this time-weary, white head."

We left him and followed a servant to a room adjoining the kitchen, where a copper basin of water had been prepared for us so that we could wash off the dust of the desert. There was no modesty between us. We stripped naked and began to lave the cool water over our bodies, using the white cotton cloths provided.

Martala breathed a sigh as she loosed the binding cloth that flattened her breasts.

"Every time I bind my breasts I feel greater discomfort."

"That's because you always have more to bind," I told her.

"What did you think about our host?" Altrus asked me.

"He is in exile; that much is obvious. Either he hides from the wrath of a powerful man, or he stays here to escape the consequence of some criminal act."

"Such was my thought, also."

Chapter 5

"*W*ake up, my love.

The murmur of Sashi's gentle voice inside my mind drew me from a dreamless slumber. Her lovely face formed itself before me in the darkness. It bore an expression of anxious concern.

What is it, Sashi? I thought.

Someone has entered the bedroom.

I listened, while keeping my breathing slow and deep, and heard the creak of a floorboard near the door. The room was so dark I could see nothing when I lifted my eyelids.

Can you see who it is?

Alas, no. When I use your eyes I can see no better in the darkness than you do.

My night vision is uncommonly keen for a human. I can distinguish the black hide of a crouching ghoul under starlight, but the room was completely dark. Whoever had entered must know the arrangement of its furniture, for he was creeping unerringly across the open floor toward the canopy bed in which I lay with Martala, who was still fast in sleep.

Pretending to groan in my dream, I rolled toward Martala so that my lips were against her ear.

"Do not move," I breathed softly. "We are being hunted."

I felt her back and neck stiffen as she came awake. We both lay listening to the stealthy approach. I was almost sure it was only a single set of bare feet that brushed the floorboards.

33

"You roll from the left side and I will roll from the right," I sighed into the girl's ear, and felt her nod against my lips.

I threw off the sheet and rolled from the bed as the unseen intruder reached the footboard. I heard Martala roll from the other side. I began to shout at the top of my lungs.

"Murder! We're being murdered! Intruders in the house! Awake, intruders in the house! Come with weapons! Murder!"

While bellowing in this asinine manner, I found the chair that held my clothing and drew my curved dagger from its ivory sheath. The rasp of the blade as it cleared its holder reassured me.

"Alhazred, I have him," Martala cried.

The sound of a struggle drew me across the floor. I heard the grit of steel against steel. I stumbled against a trunk I had forgotten was there, and by the time I reached the girl, her assailant had broken from her grasp and dashed out the door.

"Are you hurt?"

"No, not a scratch, but he has a knife. I felt the blade grind against my dagger."

"Stay in the room."

Sleep-laden voices called out from other rooms in the upper level of the house. By the time I wrapped myself in the sheet from the bed and reached the hallway, Altrus was there, carrying a flaming tinderbox. He had not taken time to light a lamp, or to put on any clothing—he stood naked apart from the dagger in his hand, the blade of which was equally exposed. Servants began to appear at the end of the hall. They cowered together, afraid to come nearer.

"He ran down the stairs and out the rear door," the mercenary told me. His voice was alert and his eyes clear, but it was always so even when he woke from a deep sleep.

"How do you know that?"

"I heard him. I'm going after him."

"Take care, he may try to lead you into a trap."

"You have a care, and don't forget your face."

He wasted no more time with words but ran down the hall and through the bewildered servants, sheltering the fluttering flame of his tinder awkwardly with the hand that held the knife.

As he passed the servants, I glimpsed their frightened faces. The Egyptian was not among them. I heard his bare feet slap the staircase, and a few moments later the bang of the back door of the house.

His warning reminded me that I had not had a chance to cast the spell of glamour that hides my disfigurement. I turned before any of the servants managed to strike a light, and used the muttered word and gesture of the spell that restores my features.

A door swung open, and Thalmus emerged into the hall with a brass lamp glowing in his hand. He wore a white sleeping gown and a matching sleeping hat with a red tassel hanging from its floppy end. Soft leather slippers covered his feet. He blinked beneath his snowy eyebrows like an irritated owl.

"What is all this shouting about murder?" he demanded of his servants.

They shrank back from his anger, and I saw in their faces that he was a hard master to serve. He turned his irritation on me.

"Someone tried to kill me and the girl in our bed. We fought him off. He ran down the stairs and out the back door."

This stopped his angry words. He studied my naked upper body with solicitude. "Are you hurt? How is the girl?"

"We are both uninjured. My man has gone after the assassin."

"Has he really? He is a brave man to go rushing out into the night."

"There is no man braver."

It was impossible to return to bed, so we dressed and descended to the sitting room to wait for Altrus. A young serving man brought us tea while we waited.

"Where is your Egyptian? I have not seen him since we awoke."

Thalmus murmured a question to the young servant, who replied in the same quiet way.

"Apparently Happisus has gone out for the evening. He was not in his room."

I looked at Martala, who nodded, but said nothing to the old man. If the thought had occurred to him that his servant might be our attacker, he chose not to voice it.

Altrus returned as we were finishing our second pot of tea. In one hand he held his extinguished tinderbox and his own dagger, and in the other he gripped a knife by the end of its ebony handle, carrying it well away from his naked body.

"Did you kill him?"

"He darted into a house. The homeowner would not open his door to me, so I could not continue my pursuit. He did drop this knife."

I came to him to examine it.

"Be careful of the blade," he said. "It may be poisoned."

Taking the knife by its handle, I turned it this way and that near the lamp. The slender, straight blade was coated with a black substance that resembled bitumen.

"Do you recognize this black matter?" I asked Thalmus.

He bent over it and sniffed it, wrinkling his long nose in displeasure.

"The tar of the black poppy."

"That is the base of the poison. It is mingled with the juices of more deadly herbs."

"Are you an expert in the brewing of poisons?" he asked in some surprise.

"Not me," I said with a slight smile. "I am merely a poor student toiling in the fields of knowledge. The expert is Fayyad al-Majid, a mage who dwells in the Lane of Scholars in Damascus. He has been kind enough to instruct me in this ancient and honored art."

"How deadly is it?" Martala asked.

I smelled the blade carefully. Beneath the tar of the poppy

I could detect at least three other ingredients, all of them fatal.

"One scratch will kill."

"Blessed Mother," she said beneath her breath. She was a worshipper of Baast, the goddess of cats, and sometimes invoked the goddess for protection. I remembered the grate of steel on steel as her tiny dagger caught the descending blade of the assassin in utter darkness.

"Has your servant, Happisus, yet returned to the house?"

"Why do you ask?"

"He may perchance have seen something in the streets."

Thalmus summoned a servant and made inquiry. The Egyptian had not returned.

"How long have you employed this man?"

Thalmus thought and shrugged his narrow shoulders inside his sleeping robe.

"Six months. My man of almost twenty years' service fell suddenly ill and died, leaving me in need of a mature overseer to regulate the work of the younger men and women of my household. By a fortunate chance, Happisus presented himself at my door seeking employment as my house-master. His references were excellent, so I hired him on the spot, and never had reason to regret it."

"Half a year," I said to Altrus. "That's about how long the agents who seek the red stone have been searching for it."

"No one could possibly have known we would come to this house," Martala pointed out.

"Would it be so hard to anticipate that whoever came after the stone would seek out its foremost authority at Jubbah?"

"I am not following your words, Alhazred," the old man said.

"Let me ask you this—has anyone else at Jubbah shown a special interest in the red stone during the past six months?"

"I don't believe so—wait, there is one man. He took a house on lease around six months ago with his grown son and daughter. A charming gentleman of refinement and culture named Fayez ibn-Kakim. He sought me out for advice on a number of occasions, and the subject of the red stone came up, but only in the most casual way during the course of our conversations. We sometimes play chess together."

"Describe the location of his house."

Thalmus sighed with vexation. I perceived that he was becoming tired. He described the location of the leased house in relation to his own. I looked at Altrus.

"It could be the one," he said. "Now I am going to bed. Whatever needs to be done can wait until morning."

Without another word he left the sitting room.

"I must do the same," Thalmus said. "I'm embarrassed to admit it, Alhazred, but I can barely keep my eyelids open."

By common accord we all returned to our beds and slept undisturbed for the remainder of the night.

Chapter 6

arly on the morrow I went with Altrus to trace the path of the assassin through the streets as he fled from the house. Martala stayed behind to question the servants, particularly the women, about Happisus, who had not returned. My suspicion was strong that the Egyptian had tried to murder me, but I wanted proof of his guilt. Altrus followed with an unerring accuracy the winding trail of the man he had pursued in darkness the previous night. We came to a back alley that led behind a house of no great pretension. The rear garden of the house was not under cultivation, and was surrounded by a wall no higher than my waist.

"He leapt over this wall like a gazelle," Altrus said. "This is where he dropped his knife. The rear door of the house was unlocked, and he vanished inside. The door was bolted by the time I reached it. I tried my shoulder on it, but the door is too strong to break."

The vision of Altrus, stark naked and with a dagger in each hand, putting his shoulder repeatedly against the door, came vividly to my mind.

"Come. We'll inquire at the front gate."

We made our way down the alley and around the wall of the house to the front, where I rang the bell at the gate.

A sullen man with a scar above his right eye answered on the fourth ring. "Whatever you're selling, we need none of it," he said with a contemptuous sneer.

"Please inform your master, Fayez ibn-Hakim, that we wish to speak with him."

"He is not expecting anyone today."

"Tell him that Thalmus sends his greetings."

The name of the elderly sage was familiar to the servant. He grunted and thought the matter over for several seconds, then turned without a word and returned to the house. He cast us a single suspicious glance before closing the front door after him.

"What do you think of this servant?" I asked Altrus.

"He's seen combat, that much is obvious. His manner is too sullen for him to be a regular soldier. I'd say he was a mercenary, and a slovenly one at that. Did you see the grease around the guard of his dagger?"

"Surely it is a mark of forethought to grease a blade against rust?"

"But it is a sign of carelessness not to wipe away the excess."

The servant returned with a silent young man at his side. The young man was dressed in a similar manner, in loose cotton work clothes, but his erect way of standing and the precision of his movements suggested military training. I noted that the younger servant also wore a dagger. It was not unheard of for servants to go armed around a household, but it was not the common practice, either.

"The master will give you ten minutes of his time," the sullen man said.

He unlocked the gate and they marched us into the house, with him in front and the younger, silent man behind us. They did not try to take our weapons, which was wise for we would not have given them.

We were shown into a room with a floor of black and white marble tiles. A man with a grey beard and a formidable nose lounged back on a divan with a book in his hand. A young man and a young woman, both around my own age, sat on cushions on the floor playing an Egyptian board game on a low table. All three were elegantly dressed.

I glanced at Altrus and inclined my head toward the young

man seated on the floor. Altrus nodded imperceptibly.

The older man shut his book with a snap and stood up with an ease and quickness that showed no ill health.

"Come in, come in. Any friends of old Thalmus are friends of mine."

"I am Abdul Alhazred, and this is my traveling companion, Altrus," I said by way of introduction.

"I am Fayez ibn-Hakim, and this is my son, Kazim, and my daughter, Najila."

The game players nodded up at us in a languid way.

"We have met before," Altrus said to Kazim.

The young man raised his eyebrows in surprise.

"I think not."

"Yesterday, in the alehouse."

Kazim shook his head. "You have mistaken me for someone else."

"You may be right," Altrus said. "I was drinking at the time."

"An honest mistake," Kazim said with a slight smile. "No harm done."

He and his sister returned their attention to their game. I had seen it played while on the Nile, but did not remember its name. It consisted of two sets of long tokens which were set into holes in the board like advancing armies. The woman's tokens were white, and she appeared to be winning, if dominance of the board was any indication. The young man's black tokens had been driven back and cornered.

"We are newcomers in Jubbah who are staying at the house of Thalmus," I said to Fayez. "The purpose of our visit is a simple one, though it may amuse you to hear it."

"Tell me, I beg you. Any source of diversion is welcome in this tedious place."

"Last night a man tried to kill me in my bed. Altrus pursued him from the house and followed him across Jubbah to your back door, which the man opened and entered. Do you know anything about this?"

He looked at his son and daughter. The young man shrugged, and the woman shook her head.

"You've beaten me again, you little cat," Kazim said to his sister, and with a careless backhand motion knocked the tokens out of their holes in the game board.

"I always beat you, brother," she said with a smile. "You have no gift of concentration."

"It appears we cannot assist you in your quest for justice," Fayez said to me. "Your friend must have confused this house with another in the darkness. Last night was moonless, I believe. It would be an easy mistake in an unfamiliar town."

"I make few mistakes," Altrus told him.

The young man laughed. Altrus looked down at him the way a leopard in a tree regards a sheep that frolics heedless in the grass below.

"Well, you must have made another one," Kazim said with a mocking smile. He glanced at his sister. "All that pounding on our back door would have awakened us, wouldn't it, Najila?"

"I'm sure it would have aroused me," she said, her eyes on my face. "I'm a very light sleeper."

"Come now, a mistake is a mistake. We'll say no more about it," Fayez put in quickly before Altrus could respond. "May I offer you a drink of wine?"

I accepted graciously. We settled ourselves in chairs and sipped the red wine when it was brought to us by the surly house attendant who had admitted us at the gate.

"What brings you to so remote an oasis, Alhazred? Surely a man of breeding and wealth could spend his days more profitably in Damascus."

"I did not mention to you that we are from Damascus."

"A lucky guess. You have the look of a man of the city, and what greater city is there in the world?"

"I might ask you the same thing. Why would an educated and cultured man of means bring his children to this remote watering hole?"

He held up his crystal glass and admired it in the beam

of sunlight that shone through a gap in the window screen and illuminated the vessel.

"That is a sad tale that I hesitate to bore you with. Suffice it to say that my dear wife of twenty-three years died quite suddenly, leaving me bereft of any comfort. I brought my children here to heal the wound in my heart and to recover my joy in life."

"It is indeed an admirable retreat for one who wishes to escape from the vicissitudes of the world. Thalmus tells me that you are a scholar."

"I dabble," Fayez said. "The study of ancient history distracts my mind from its sorrows."

"I, too, am something of a scholar. I hope to learn more about the ancient history of Jubbah, and of the people that once lived here."

"Do you speak of the Thamud?"

"Indeed, I do."

"How curious that we both should have an interest in that strange tribe of cliff dwellers. My children and I spend much of our time walking about on Jabal Umm Sanman, searching for relics of that forgotten people."

"It is my intention to explore the mountain as well."

"Are you not intimidated by the legends?"

"What legends are those?"

"The Bedouins are afraid of the mountain. They believe it is haunted by a djinn with black wings and fearsome claws. Very few of them will go up there."

"On the contrary, such a legend gives me hope that the mountain holds undisturbed evidence concerning the mysterious fate of that ancient people."

He shook his head sadly at me.

"I fear you will be disappointed. We have combed the mountain and have found so little, it is scarcely worth talking about. A few bone tools, some rock drawings."

"I expect you are correct. It is surely futile for me to cover the same ground that you have already covered. Even so, I intend to amuse myself by walking about on the mountain."

"No doubt we will encounter each other from time to time," he said.

"I hope we don't mistake you for bandits," his son said in a mild voice. "It would be terrible if we were to shoot you with arrows before we recognized who you are."

"Are there many bandits around the oasis?"

"Not many, but enough to use caution when venturing away from the walls of the town," Fayez said.

"I always carry my bow with me," the young woman told me. "I'm quite a good shot with it."

"We will try to alert you to our presence if we spy you on the rocks," I assured them.

With smiles and pleasant words, we left the house of Fayez and headed back to the house of Thalmus.

"Did you see the smirk on the lips of that pup?" Altrus grumbled.

"Our presence seemed to amuse all three of them," I said. "Of course they were lying."

"Of course."

"I doubt very much if they are related by blood."

"The way that pup leered at his sister and caressed the back of her hand, it would be an outrage against nature if they were siblings."

"They are mercenaries, all of them."

Martala came running out to open the gate of Thalmus's house when we rang the brass bell.

"There has been news since you left," she said with some excitement. "Happisus has been found."

"Where?" Altrus demanded.

"He was found amid the graves at the place of burial outside the oasis. His throat was cut."

Chapter 7

The burial ground for Jubbah was far enough away from the walls of the town to avoid contamination of its well water, or so the people of the oasis hoped. It was located on a low ridge and had no bordering stone wall of the kind that is usually found around graveyards. Some of the graves were ancient and others comparatively recent. It was obvious to my practiced eye that it had been in continuous use for centuries. During the time I spent as a ghoul I had occasion to frequent many places of the dead. There was sure to be a clan of ghouls at Jubbah, and the most likely place for their warrens was beneath this burial ground.

We found a dozen men standing around the corpse, which had not yet been raised from its place. Two stood some distance away with a handcart at the ready. I assumed it was to be used to retrieve the body. Most of the men were mere curious onlookers, but one among them seemed to be in command. He pushed the gawkers further away from the corpse, which lay on its back with a red splash of dried blood across its throat and down the front of its sleeveless white vest. It was Happisus, and he had been dead for hours.

Altrus pressed through the crowd and squatted to study the body.

"I told you, get away from there," the officious man said. "This isn't a marketplace."

He reached to grasp Altrus by the shoulder, but a hard

glance from the mercenary stayed his hand. Altrus slowly straightened his legs.

"Who are you, to tell me what I can look at?"

The other man drew himself up to his full height, which was somewhat below average.

"I am Trievos, appointed by the mayor of Jubbah, the honorable Hafiz ibd Ahmad, to enforce the rule of law at the oasis. If you were not outsiders you would know this."

"We mean no offense," I said in a mild voice, stepping forward between them. I didn't want Altrus to kill the fool before I had a chance to talk to him.

"Well, now you know, so there can be no excuse in future."

"We are staying at the house of the scholar Thalmus, and we heard that his Egyptian servant Happisus had been found dead in the burial ground. We came to verify the truth of this rumor, so that we could give a correct report to Thalmus."

This seemed to make sense to him. He nodded and grunted.

"Just do not touch the body until I have had the opportunity to study the ground around and beneath it."

"It appears this man met his death by having his throat slashed from behind."

"Why do you say from behind?" He eyed me suspiciously.

"Look at the length of the cut. It wraps halfway around his neck. A knife slash from the front makes a shorter cut."

He nodded. "You have a good eye," he said reluctantly.

"There's another point, which I'm sure you have already observed."

"Perhaps I have," he said, "but you tell me anyway."

I pointed at the rocks and sand around the head of the corpse.

"There is almost no blood on the ground. Wherever this man was killed, it was not in the graveyard."

He nodded again. "Such was my surmise as well."

"Have you examined the corpse for possessions?"

"Not yet, but I will do so now."

He bent and opened Happisus's purse, then emptied out

its contents onto the palm of his hand. The purse contained half a dozen silver coins.

"Whatever the reason for his murder, it wasn't robbery," Martala muttered.

She was wearing the trailing end of her kufiya over the lower part of her face, and it concealed her long hair coiled beneath it. Her breasts were bound, which gave her the body profile of a gangling youth. Trievos ignored her words as he would the words of any child.

He felt inside the vest for pockets but found nothing. Then he twisted the belt around the waist of the corpse to expose the empty sheath of a dagger. He tipped the corpse this way and that to view the ground beneath it.

"His dagger is missing. That's probably the weapon that killed him," he muttered.

Bending down, he sniffed at the empty sheath, which has a crusting of black tar around the brass plate at its top.

"What is it you smell?" I asked.

He shook his head. "I don't know. Some kind of drug, perhaps."

"Why do you think he was killed?"

He made a gesture of disgust with his hand, as though throwing something away.

"It is useless to speculate. He may have been drunk, and found himself embroiled in a dispute over a dice game, or a woman. If so, he was murdered in the heat of passion, and his killers decided to move his corpse here to turn suspicion away from themselves."

He motioned for the men with the handcart to wheel it close. They loaded the corpse upon it with some difficulty, as the limbs had gone rigid.

"What will you do now?" I asked Trievos.

"The body will be delivered back to Thalmus, who can make whatever arrangements regarding its disposal he wishes. I will ask the usual questions in the usual places. I do not expect anyone to volunteer useful information, but it is a part of my duties to be thorough in seeking out the truth."

"Suppose it were to fall out that the murder was done by a man of wealth and influence?" I asked.

He glared at me as though I had questioned his integrity.

"It is my duty to report my findings to the mayor and his council. After that the matter is out of my hands."

We watched him return toward the walls of Jubbah with the cart and the onlookers, who had exhausted their curiosity. The wind blew up and raised little eddies of dust between the headstones. The scent of blood lingered on the air.

"One thing puzzles me," Altrus said. "If there are ghouls at Jubbah, why did they not take the corpse during the night?"

"It was too fresh," I explained. "Ghouls cannot digest fresh meat. It gives them stomach cramps, and since they are unable to vomit, the pain is almost unbearable. Left out for a day, exposed to the sun, the corpse would have been fit to eat. But don't worry, after it is buried here they will come and claim what is theirs."

The expression of revulsion on his face, and on the face of the girl, amused me. During the time I lived among the Black Spring Clan of ghouls in the Empty Space, I had eaten meat from many corpses of men, women and children. It was that, or death. I chose to live. The prospect of eating the Egyptian after his flesh had aged in the sun did not disgust me. Truth be spoken, it gave an edge to my appetite. It was many months since I had eaten like a ghoul. The memories of the feasts in which I had participated as part of the Black Spring Clan made me stroke the skull of Gor that hung at my belt with sadness. I missed the sense of community and fellowship, the banter of words and the easy laughter.

"It may be that the ghouls of this clan can give me some sense of what took place here."

"It was Fayez or his son that killed him, most likely as soon as I retreated from their back door," Altrus asserted with confidence.

"I have no doubt that you are correct. Even so, I will return here after sundown and learn what I can."

"Do you want me to come with you?" Altrus asked.

I laughed out loud before I could stop myself, and patted him on the shoulder.

"There is boldness in your offer, but they would kill you before you spoke five words, and you would not even see them coming. No, I must go alone."

Martala said nothing during this exchange, a period of quiet that was uncharacteristic for her. She stood on one of the headstones and shaded her eyes to peer across the plain to the east.

"What are you looking at?" I asked.

She pointed with her finger.

"See there? Near the horizon."

"It's a dust devil," I said indifferently. "The desert is filled with them."

"I know that," she said. "Why doesn't it move?"

I looked again, this time with greater interest. The three of us stood for a while like statues with our hands at our foreheads to block the light of the sky from our eyes so that we could see more detail. The turning column of dusty air undulated and danced, but did not move from its place. It was a thing I had never seen before. Dust devils always moved. They were borne on the wind and made of air. They could not remain fixed, yet there it was, spinning like a lathe with its point set into the ground.

Then, as though the dust devil had become aware of our attention, it wavered, thinned, and vanished in a fall of sand.

"They say dust devils are the djinn of the desert," Martala murmured.

"They say rightly," I told her. "But most of the time, they are just dust."

We continued to stare uneasily across the plain for several minutes before turning our steps back to the town gate.

49

Chapter 8

"I drew up this map for your use this morning," Thalmus told me. We were in his study, bent over his desk. "It shows the principal pathways up the mountain, and the places of interest that I have found in the course of my decades of wandering. There is even a spring of water that flows forth sometimes after the rains. It may be flowing today."

"I thank you for this," I said, rolling the map up and sliding it inside the open neck of my tunic to one of the pockets that I had instructed the tailor at Damascus to sew into the garment.

"It was the least I could do to make amends, after my servant tried to kill you."

"We won't stay on the mountain for very long today. I just want to make a preliminary exploration."

"To think that I could have been deceived by Happisus for so many months," he said, shaking his white head.

"Don't torment yourself. He was planted in your household by Fayez and his people on the assumption that someone else might come from Damascus searching for the stone. You are well known as the preeminent authority on the Thamud tribe. It was a natural assumption that anyone coming to Jubbah to look for the stone would seek you out."

"I am shocked by what you say about Fayez. I played shatranj with the man on many occasions, and never did I sense dishonor in him."

"He may well be an honorable man, in his own way, but

do not be deceived by him. He is prepared to kill to get what he seeks, and to prevent others from getting it."

The old man took my hand and patted it.

"I wish I could come with you, Alhazred, but I fear my days of climbing the mountain are over. My legs are not what they once were, you know."

"I understand, Thalmus. This map should provide all the guidance we need."

I started to pull my hand away, but he held it.

"Have a care on the mountain. It is a strange place, ancient beyond the memory of man, and there are things that dwell there that are not natural."

"What kinds of things?"

He released my fingers and shrugged.

"Who knows. I have seen things in the twilight—misshapen figures between the rocks, moving shadows where no shadows should be, falling stones when there was no reason for them to fall—and I have heard distant voices speaking in a language that is not any tongue of man."

"We will take care," I assured him.

I left his study. Martala and Altrus waited for me in the front hall.

"How was he?" the girl asked.

"The betrayal of his trust by Happisus has shaken him. He is old and frail. I fear he has not many years left in this world, or perhaps not many months."

We left the house and passed through the streets of the town, which was somewhat more subdued than usual beneath the heat of the noonday sun. I carried a waterskin over my shoulder on its long strap. Altrus and the girl carried similar skins. They had not wanted to bear them because of their weight, but I had insisted on it. Any man who ventures into the desert without water is a fool. That we intended to be away from Jubbah only for a few hours did not change these realities.

For a time we walked along the base of the mountain, which rose up from the flat plain in a startling manner, like the shoulder of a sleeping giant. I located the place on Thalmus's map that indicated the start of a trail that led up the slope, and we began the long climb. Progress was not easy. There was almost no flat ground on the mountain. We were climbing up, or we were climbing down. The only respite was when we made a precarious transit of a ridge, with a fatal fall threatening us on both sides.

"Look, there is one of the rock carvings Thalmus told us about," Martala said.

We approached the side of a great boulder and studied the faint markings. There were stick figures of human beings, camels, horses, even a wagon, and some writing in Arabic characters.

"What does it say?" Altrus asked.

I studied the writing for a time, then nodded my head.

"Something about coming here with camels. There are a few names. I think it must have been carved by Bedouin."

"How old do you think it is?"

"Not old. A hundred years, perhaps. Maybe two hundred. Not old."

Altrus laughed and shook his head in disgust.

"Why do you laugh?"

"If all the rock carvings are as meaningless as this one, how are we to find the red stone? Fayez and his party have searched the mountain for the past six months. Thalmus has been looking for it for many years. What chance do we have?"

"Not much," I admitted. "But we need to make an honest attempt. I promised Muawiya."

"This is a fool's errand," he muttered.

We continued on along the trail, which was so faint as to be invisible in places, and over the next two hours found half a dozen more carvings at various elevations. Nothing depicted on the stones cast any illumination about the fate of the Thamud or the resting place of the red stone. The sun was declining in a cloudless western sky when I decided to call an end to our first exploratory trek on the mountain.

I led the way for a time, stopped, and took out Thalmus's map to study it.

"What's wrong?" Martala asked

"I believe we've walked this way before."

"We have," Altrus said. "I recognize that outcropping over there."

I continued on, growing ever more frustrated. The trail had ceased to conform to any feature on the map. Only the sun, which dropped ever lower, gave me a sense of which direction we were taking. We were lost amid buttresses and knife-edged ridges of stone. The plain was not visible. I had only a general sense where Jubbah lay, and there seemed no way to go in that direction without meeting obstacles that forced us into long and tortuous detours.

Altrus sidled toward me when we stopped to rest and take water.

"We're lost, aren't we," he said.

"Nonsense. I know exactly where the damned mountain is."

He laughed gently.

"This map is worthless," I said in disgust. "I should have known better than to depend on it."

"Even if we have to spend the night up here, it's no great tragedy," he said.

"We'll be cold."

"I've been cold before. We can huddle together for warmth."

"Hush; listen." I held up my hand.

In the silence came the sound of a distant voice. It was faint but clear. It seemed to be chanting something. I could not recognize any words. The voice continued for less than a minute, then stopped.

"Did either of you recognize the language?"

Both shook their heads solemnly.

In some subtle way the atmosphere of the mountain had transitioned from indifferent to hostile. I could not have said how it occurred, but I felt it in the pit of my stomach as a sinking feeling and as a prickling on the back of my bare neck. We were being watched.

In frustration, I cast the map away.

"We will guide ourselves by the sun—what's left of it." The redly glowing orb had almost hidden itself behind the tumbled boulders.

Neither of my companions made any comment, but I saw Altrus test the looseness of his sword in its scabbard.

The trail seemed strange to my eyes. This might be only because I was retracing it in the opposite direction, and all of the views that opened before me were the reverse of what I had seen while hiking into the mountain. Or it might be so because it was not the same trail.

The others did not grumble or argue with my choice of directions. They cast their gaze all around the thrusting rocky shoulders and ridges, alert for any danger.

"Alhazred, look behind," Martala called sharply.

I turned in time to see a kind of shadow slide along the rocks and vanish behind an outcropping.

"What was it?" Altrus demanded.

"Didn't you see it?"

"No."

I described the shadow to him.

"Something must have walked along a ridge and cast its shadow down on the rocks. A desert fox, perhaps."

"That is possible," I said, but I was not convinced.

The distant chanting in the strange tongue began again, rising and falling as the breeze carried it toward our ears or away. We stood listening until it stopped.

"I don't want to spend the night on this mountain," Martala murmured.

I made no response, but gritted my teeth in frustration. According to the sun at my back, I was moving in a prevailing easterly direction, although it was completely impossible to walk in a straight line over those sinuous ridges and ravines. We should be moving toward the oasis, but there was still no glimpse ahead of any green, nor for that matter of the plain itself.

An arrow struck the waterskin hanging beneath my arm. I felt and heard its impact before I realized what had hit me. It was a sharp little dig at my ribs that hurt, but not greatly.

Altrus pulled the girl down behind a boulder and I quickly followed.

"Are you hurt?"

Lifting off the leather bag, I saw that it was pierced on both sides. Water trickled out each hole. The sharp point of the arrow had also pierced my tunic and undershirt. There was blood on its point.

Martala helped me draw up the long skirt of my tunic through my belt to examine my wound. The arrowhead had penetrated into the flesh over my ribs no more than a finger's breadth. I worked the shaft out of my waterskin and examined the head closely, smelling it and turning it to catch the redness of the dying sun on its edges.

"Poisoned?" Altrus asked.

"I think not."

He nodded and gripped the hilt of his sword in its sheath.

"I saw the place from which it was fired. Stay under cover. I won't be long."

Without waiting for a response, he withdrew back between the rocks, keeping his back bent and his head low.

"The blood is stopping," Martala said as she continued to examine my wound.

"The tip of the arrow struck a rib. Most of its force was spent anyway."

I studied the dart more closely. It was stained black with a dull finish that would not flash in the sunlight. The black fletching looked like crow feathers. The shaft was somewhat shorter than the usual hunting arrow, suggesting that it had been fired from the bow of a youth, or a woman. Had it been treated with the same poison that was on Hippisus's dagger, I would already be dead.

"We must keep moving," I told the girl. "We cannot afford to let the bowman find his angle."

"Or the bow-woman," Martala murmured.

56

I remembered Najila bragging about her skill with a bow, but I made no comment.

We kept our heads low and moved quickly from cover to cover, acutely conscious of the few seconds when we were fully exposed to the hills behind us. I expected a second arrow but it did not come. A rattle of loose stones made us draw our weapons. I stood with my sword naked in my hand. The girl had her little dagger at the ready. Its broad blade was no more than a handbreadth in length, but she refused to carry anything larger.

Altrus came into view. He grinned at us when he saw our steel.

"The bowman escaped."

"Did you see him?"

"No, but I heard him scramble over the rocks. He was moving higher up the mountain and must have known the way, for he moved faster than I could follow."

We continued on the course I had chosen, all of us alert for any sound or movement in the still air of twilight. Just as I was about to admit that I was hopelessly lost, we emerged onto the shoulder of the mountain, and I realized I had found the way back to the same trail by which we had ascended hours earlier. We made our weary way to Jubbah through the gathering gloom.

... starlight reflected from black claws and bared fangs.

Chapter 9

The thin crescent of the waxing moon, like a silver bow drawn by an invisible archer, had already set by the time I returned to the burial ground. I was alone. I sat on a rounded headstone and waited. Sooner or later they would come. They could not afford to pass up the chance for so much meat. Ghouls cannot eat a freshly killed corpse, but they had no compunction about committing murder and then hiding the body where it could decay into something upon which they could feast. I should know. I had done the same myself while living as a member of the Black Spring Clan in the Empty Space.

When they began to gather behind me, I sensed it rather than heard them. No beast can move as silently as a ghoul in the night. I waited for them to draw near, then stood and turned to face them with my hand on the hilt of my dagger.

"Is that any way to greet a ghoul from the Black Spring Clan?" I asked in the ghoul language.

The burial ground appeared empty, but I could see starlight reflected from black claws and bared fangs.

"Where is the hospitality of your clan? Or do you mean to slay one of your own brothers?"

A hissing laughter came forth from the darkness. It was disquietingly close.

"You are human, not ghoul. We do not talk to our food."

"I am Alhazred of the Black Spring Clan, a ghoul who has hunted with ghouls and shared the feast." A pebble rolled behind me. "Tell your foolish youngling that if he takes another step, I will cut his throat."

The ghoul who stood before me hissed a word in their guttural tongue, and the youth who had tried to creep up behind me so unskilfully withdrew, making more noise than he had made in his approach.

"Forgive him," the ghoul before me said through the darkness. "He is the child of my mate's sister. Her family is not gifted."

I let my dagger slide back into its sheath. He moved forward, and suddenly I saw his outline. He was large and well-muscled, which was to be expected of a clan that dwelled in such a lush land with so much potential food on the caravan roads. My clanmates at the Black Spring had been smaller and leaner of body, the result of chronic starvation. I wondered if this ghoul had ever been hungry, as I had been.

He sniffed the air, crouching and then raising his dog-like snout with its pronounced canines.

"You smell like man, not ghoul."

Untying the skull that swung at my belt, I held it out to him.

"Does this smell like man?"

He put his face so near, I felt the warmth of the breath from his flared black nostrils. Even so near, he was almost invisible in the darkness. The skin of a ghoul is like black velvet and reflects no light.

"How did you get this skull?" There was hostility in his tone. The others behind him sensed it and inched forward.

"He was my friend," I said quickly. "His name was Gor, and he was leader of the Black Spring Clan. I wear his skull out of love for him."

The ghoul hesitated, then withdrew his jaws, which had been near my fingertips.

"Is he the one who took you into his clan?"

"He is. Without the hospitality of Gor I would not be alive."

This comment seemed to satisfy him. He nodded.

"My name is Bakka. I accept that you are a ghoul of the Black Spring Clan, and I offer you the sanctuary and hospitality of the Green Earth Clan."

For the first time since sensing his presence, I took a full breath and relaxed my body.

"Come with us, Alhazred. We will eat and talk."

I followed the ghouls, who were five in number and all males, to a remote corner of the burial ground where only a few of the oldest graves were located.

"You move well, for a man," Bakka said with approval.

"It was Gor who taught me how to move in darkness."

They slid aside two flat stones, revealing a hole that at first sight appeared too narrow for any creature larger than a jackal. This first look was deceptive. One by one the ghouls slid into the hole head first, leaving only me and Bakka beneath the stars.

"Slide in; there is more room below," he said.

I did not hesitate. While entering the hole I would be completely vulnerable if they chose to attack me, but the thought did not even arise. The word of a ghoul is his bond, and Bakka had given me hospitality. I knelt and fitted my arms into the hole, made my shoulders as narrow as possible, and turned my head to the side. In a moment I had fallen down a short chute and into an open chamber that was almost high enough to stand in.

An oil lamp burned in a hollow in the earthen wall. Ghouls have extremely sensitive eyes, but they are not able to see in total darkness. As I had expected, all four of the ghouls who surrounded me were naked, or nearly so. Two of them wore leather belts with bags and tools attached to them. None of them carried knives—their talons and their teeth were their weapons. All were adorned with bits of jewelry, such as bracelets and rings in their ears. If ghouls have any vanity, it is for jewelry, which the males favor more than the females. Above their body odor, which was not unpleasant to me, I smelled the scent of damp soil. The walls and floor of the warren were not dripping, but they were not completely dry, either. It was a consequence of living on the edge of an oasis.

Bakka extended his feet from the hole of the roof, and another ghoul stood so that his feet rested on the ghoul's sloped shoulders. I realized Bakka must be moving the rocks back over the hole. He dropped into the chamber and shook off the loose soil like a dog.

"Come with me to the main hall," he said.

I followed him through dimly-illuminated tunnels with my legs bent and my head lowered. We emerged into a long room where I could stand straight. Down its center ran several slabs of flat stone raised from the floor by stone blocks to make a table. Animal skins lay along the floor on either side, and here and there ghouls sat upon them. They eyed me with curiosity when I entered the hall, especially the children. Bakka explained who I was, and the clan accepted his words without dispute or reluctance.

He spoke to an elderly female. She grinned and went away to another part of the warren.

"Sit, sit," he said, coiling his powerful legs beneath him.

I sat beside him at the table with my legs crossed. Around us gathered twenty or thirty young male ghouls who I took to be Bakka's best warriors. They eyed me with appraisal, wondering how difficult it would be to kill me. I did not blame them for this—I was wondering how many of them I could kill should they attack me.

The old female came back with two younger she-ghouls, who bore between them a flat stone on which rested the torso of a human being that had been split open from its throat to its groin. The organs and intestines were laid bare between the gaping ribs. From their smell and color, I could tell they were about five days old. That is to say, the person who had possessed this torso had died five days ago.

The females laid the slab on the table in front of us with toothy grins.

"Eat, eat," Bakka said, eying me from the corner of his eye.

This was hospitality, but it was also a test. I had declared myself a ghoul. Only a ghoul could partake of this feast without being sickened. Should I fail to eat the meat offered to me, or should I vomit it up, they would kill me without an instant's hesitation.

I dug my hand into the abdominal cavity of the torso and took out a length of small intestine. With some difficulty I broke off a section that was about a cubit in length and began to gnaw the end.

Bakka watched for a time, then relaxed and nodded his approval. He pulled the heart from the rotting carcass and tore off a chunk of it, chewing with gusto. The other ghouls reached into the torso and tore out whatever meat they wanted, taking turns in order according to their status in the clan. The females brought forth clay jugs of the fermented drink ghouls use for wine and poured it into clay cups.

The taste of the decaying flesh was familiar. It carried me back in time to my months of life with the Black Spring clan. Feasts such as this were rare for my old clan, which, alas! was no more. A merchant of a caravan, enraged that the ghouls of my clan would dig up and eat the corpse of his newly dead daughter, poisoned her flesh out of malice. Only I survived the feast, because I was able to vomit forth the tainted meat. Ghouls cannot vomit.

"I should never have doubted you, Alhazred," Bakka said, slapping me on the shoulder in the rough camaraderie of ghouls.

"It is long since I have eaten so well," I told him, and meant it. Human flesh is an acquired taste, but once acquired is not easily abandoned.

When everyone had eaten and drunk his fill, I opened to Bakka the reason for my visit to his hunting ground. He listened with attention, nodding from time to time.

"I know the house of which you speak. It was vacant a long time before it was given to Fayez and his pups. They go walking on the mountain almost every day, but they return before dark with nothing to show for it."

"I believe they sent the Egyptian servant to kill me so that I would not find the thing they seek."

63

"The magic rock," he said.

"I don't know if it is truly magic, but people believe it is, and that gives it power over the affairs of men."

"Men are strange creatures," he said, shaking his head. "I do not pretend to understand them."

"Nor do I."

"My hunters saw the servants of this Fayez carry the corpse of the Egyptian to the burial place. I was tempted to drag the corpse beneath the ground to rot, but some caution made me leave it on the surface."

"It is well you did. The body will be buried on the morrow, and then it will be yours in any case."

"So it has always been. Men consign their dead to the earth, and the earth yields them up to ghouls."

I shifted my seat so that I could face him more directly.

"The reason I came was to ask if you know of any lore concerning the red stone or the ancient people that kept it."

He motioned for an elderly ghoul to approach and sit beside him on his other side. The old ghoul whispered into his pointed ear for several minutes, from time to time rolling his bloodshot eye in my direction.

"We know of no lore other than what is common knowledge among men," he said. "The red stone was brought to the oasis by an ancient race of humans who built their houses and temples into the sides of the mountains. What became of them, or the red stone, is not known to us."

My heart fell, but I nodded, trying not to betray my disappointment. The memory of ghoul clans is long. Ghouls remember much curious lore that has been forgotten by men. I had hoped for some information that would give me an advantage over Fayez.

"Have you talked with the witch of the mountain?" Bakka asked.

"Is there a witch on Jabal Umm Sanman?" I asked in surprise.

"For as long as any ghoul can remember. She lives in a cave near the summit of the mountain, or so it is said, and is fabled among ghouls to be immortal."

"How may I find this cave?"

He shrugged and shook his head in apology.

"No one knows exactly where it is. But I can tell you her name."

"Please, tell it."

"She calls herself Salamagoogah."

I repeated it aloud so that I would remember it.

"That is a strange name. It almost has a djinn sound to it."

He nodded in agreement. The djinn were known to favor long and complex names for themselves.

"It is said that she ventures forth on the mountain only at twilight, either in the mornings or the evenings. She wears a black dress or cloak that covers her entire body, and her face is veiled with a black veil. No one has ever seen her features."

"What of the red stone itself? Can you tell me nothing about it?"

He murmured to the aged advisor, who whispered back.

"Only that the stone is fabled to be an evil thing that must never be touched."

Chapter 10

When I returned to Jubbah, it was some time after midnight. The village was silent apart from the occasional bark of a dog. Martala met me at the wrought-iron gate of Thalmus's house. She was fully dressed.

"After you left for the burial ground, Altrus went out. He said he was going to learn more about Feyez and his men. He wouldn't let me go with him, but said he would be back in an hour or two."

"When was this?"

"Six hours ago."

"Altrus can take care of himself," I told her. "We should go to bed. He will return when he is ready."

"No," she said. "I have a bad feeling in my heart. You know me, Alhazred. I have the second sight. Something has gone wrong, and Altrus needs us."

I knew her well enough to realize the futility of arguing with her. If I did not accompany her on her search, she would go alone, and no words of mine would stop her.

"Very well, our soft bed can wait. We will look for Altrus."

She went with me as I turned from the gate and made my way down the empty street.

"Where should we look first?" she asked.

"You know Altrus as well as I do. Like as not, he went to an alehouse that has women and gambling, and got himself shut in for the night."

The alehouses were compelled to close by a certain hour.

This did not prevent some of the more disreputable houses from continuing to serve their customers behind their locked doors. Once locked in for the night, the men inside could drink, whore and gamble, but they could not leave until the door was unlocked at dawn. It would have been natural for Altrus to make the rounds of the alehouses and whore houses seeking gossip about Feyez and his men, and it would have been natural for him to become drunk and lose track of the time.

The first two signs under which we stopped were quiet within. We continued into the worst quarter of the town, where most of the beggars and criminals no doubt resided. The streets were dark. I took the hand of the girl and guided her along behind me. I could make out the outlines of buildings by starlight, but I knew she saw nothing in the darkness. We passed hooded and silent individuals who drew back from us, and once encountered a group of three drunkards with a lantern. They began to approach with knives and clubs in their hands to rob us, but when they saw the gleam of my sword, they fell silent and passed on the other side of the street with nothing more hostile than sullen looks.

I stopped beneath a third sign, and heard the murmur of voices and laughter through the door.

"Do you think Altrus is in there?" Martala asked.

"Who can know? If he is not in this one, he must be in another like it."

She put her hand on the door, then laid her cheek against it.

"I think he is here. I feel his presence."

Drawing my dagger, I pounded on the door with the heavy brass knob on the end of its hilt. After a time a small shutter opened in the door, spilling lamplight into the street.

"Go away," said a harsh male voice. "Can't you see we're closed for the night?"

"You lie. I can hear people inside. Let me in or I will raise a din and wake the entire town."

The shutter slammed shut. I waited a few seconds, then began to pound on the door. It finally opened to a wave of laughter and applause from the drunken patrons inside.

"Come in, then, you lout," the doorman said. "But know this: the door won't be opened again until sunrise."

"That's good enough for us," I said as I shoved past him. "My young companion and I want to get drunk and throw the dice."

The air inside was warm and moist, laden with a dozen undesirable smells in which one predominated. It was the natural result of forcing too many drunken bodies into too small an enclosed space. The sweat and exhalation of a drunkard has a peculiar stench that once smelled can never be forgotten, and the air of this alehouse was thick with it. Here and there, men sat slumped over tables or lay on the straw of the floor in puddles of their own vomit, snoring lustily. We moved deeper into the room, past a flight of stairs that no doubt led up to the bedrooms of the whores.

The alehouse had two chambers on the lower level that were connected by a large archway. The dice game was taking place in the back room on an open space on the floor of beaten mud, with the wall for a backdrop. Six of the more alert patrons were throwing the dice while another dozen or so men and a few harlots watched in varying stages of drunkenness. Altrus was one of the dice players. His eye roved across us as we entered but he gave no sign of recognition.

I went to the bar and loudly demanded ale for myself and the girl. There was no point in trying to pass unnoticed, so I played the part of a drunkard. We stood watching Altrus throw the dice. He lost and cursed creatively. I observed that he was not nearly as intoxicated as his slurred speech would suggest. His movements were precise and his charcoal eyes keen.

One of the young men watching on the other side of the dice floor was a servant of Fayez. He met my gaze but gave no sign of recognition. I had a sense that some drama was transpiring at my feet but I could not guess what it might be.

"Damn you all, I've lost all my silver," Altrus muttered as he pushed himself awkwardly to his feet.

The other players laughed at him and the game continued. He lurched toward me. What he intended to say was lost when the front door of the alehouse burst inward. I turned and saw Trievos rush forward with two of his town guards. Beside him was another man who was dressed like a merchant. I recognized the surly countenance of the servant with the scar over his right eye who had admitted us to Fayez's house.

"That's the man," he cried, pointing his finger at Altrus. "That's the man who cheated me."

The drunken pose fell away from Altrus.

"What are you talking about?"

"His dice were weighted," the man said. "He robbed me. I demand justice."

The other servant of Fayez stepped forward.

"He speaks the truth. I saw it. This man with the burn mark on his cheek used loaded dice and took all his money. Look, there are his two accomplices. They are all in on it together."

He pointed at me.

Trievos narrowed his eyes.

"The five of you will have to come with me. I will need to question each of you separately."

"Is there a back way out of this place?" I murmured to Altrus as I leaned near.

"Yes."

It was like him to have already verified the existence of a rear exit.

"Take the girl and get out of here," I told him.

"No, you take the girl. I will stay and slow them down."

"Do as I tell you," I said harshly.

He did not argue, but glared at me as he stepped past me to take Martala by the arm.

I knew what was coming. We were puppets in a market

show. The patrons of the alehouse and Trievos were to be our audience.

The older servant of Fayez with the scar, who had entered with the magistrate, drew his sword and rushed toward me.

"He's trying to get away. Stop the thief!"

He would have run me through had I not drawn my own weapon and parried his thrust. The drunkards and their whores milled about in confusion, trying to get out of the way of the blades.

"Put up your swords," Trievos bellowed above the noise.

The servant ignored him. I felt the other man coming toward me from the side and stepped back until my shoulders touched the wall. I could not spare a glance to see what had become of Altrus or the girl, but I had confidence he would get her out and away safely.

The young man creeping from the side made the mistake of over-extending his lunge. I put my sword's point through his heart. At the same moment Trievos used his sword to beat down the weapon of the other servant, and his men grabbed both of us and took away our weapons.

"Well, you've killed him," Trievos said in disgust after examining the body on the floor. "This is a more serious crime than cheating at dice."

"I never even picked up the dice," I told him. "Ask these witnesses."

My witnesses were rapidly slipping out the open front door and into the street with furtive looks. None of them appeared interested in testifying in my defense.

"It was all planned," Fayez's remaining servant said. "The three of them were in on it together. They are all guilty."

Altrus and the girl were nowhere to be seen. I knew they would make their way back to Thalmus's house.

"You'll have to come with me," Trievos said. "I must confine you until I can get this affair sorted out."

He escorted me and Fayez's servant to the town jail, a small building with stone walls, an iron-bound door, and a single barred window. We were thrust inside the darkness together.

"Sleep off the effects of your drink," he said to us in a voice of contempt as he slammed shut the door. "I will question you both in the morning."

I heard the brass lock rattle when he turned the key.

Chapter 11

The jail cell was far from the worst place I've had to sleep. In the momentary flash of light from the lantern Trievos held, I had seen that the straw on the floor was dirty and infested with fleas. They jumped as the light played over them. Filthy sleeping rugs lay on this straw on opposite sides of the room, which was about five paces in each dimension. Apart from an elderly man who lay curled up on another sleeping rug, unconscious and shivering with his arms hugged around his shoulders, we were the only prisoners. In the corner rested a clay pitcher and a clay pot with a lid. All this I saw before the lantern was withdrawn.

In the darkness, I walked over to investigate what was in the pitcher and found it to be water that was fit to drink but none too clean. The purpose for the pot was apparent as soon as I raised its lid.

Fayez's servant said nothing. I could feel his eyes seeking out the shadow of my form through the darkness. The delirious mumbles of the old man were loud in the stillness.

"Why did you try to kill me?"

He grunted in derision. "The plan was to get your mercenary arrested and imprisoned here."

"You have no witnesses. None of the people who were in the alehouse will testify against me."

"They will testify as they are told to testify, and be well paid for it."

"So that's the way it is."

"You should have left Jubbah while you had the chance."

I stretched myself out on my sleeping rug. I heard him do the same on the opposite side of the cell. It was cold on the floor. I was glad I had eaten with the ghouls. At least I was not hungry.

After a time the other man feigned to snore. I was not deceived.

Keep watch for me, Sashi, I thought.

Her lovely oval face floated on the darkness as she nodded. *Of course, my love.*

I fell into a light sleep. At some point in the hours before dawn Sashi woke me. *He comes to you, Alhazred.*

Keeping my breathing regular, I prepared my body and waited. He had no weapon, but he had taken off his headscarf and held the length of its cloth between his fists. I discovered this when he tried to wrap it around my throat. He was hindered by the thickness of the cloth and the darkness. I did not struggle to escape but drew him down upon me and bit his throat. The taste of his warm blood as it gushed over my lips was not unpleasant. He struggled for a time but I held him like a lover. When he was dead, I pushed him off me. The stench of fresh blood filled the air. The old man had not awakened, but continued to shiver and mumble.

At least I will not starve, I thought, and laughed to myself. It was a foolish thought. Naturally they would take the body away, when they discovered it in the morning. Still, there was always the old man to fall back on, if the need arose. This comforted me.

"Alhazred, are you in there?"

It was Altrus outside the barred window. I stood and went over to him.

"You smell like a slaughterhouse," he said.

"Fayez's man tried to kill me. How is the girl?"

"When I left her, she was asleep, or at least pretending to be asleep. I made her promise not to leave the house."

"Good. Fayez has decided to move against us. I want her safe."

"I'll keep her safe."

"I know you will."

He tested the iron bars with his hands, but they did not move so much as a hair's breadth.

"It would take a team of oxen to rip these out."

"Never mind that." I put my hands over his. There was the hint of daylight in the eastern sky. I could see the outline of his head, but not his face. "I want you to stay away from Trievos and his guards. He may be an honest magistrate but until we know this for certain, treat him as an enemy. If you need to leave Thalmus's house, you may be able to buy sanctuary among the Bedouins."

"Is there anything I can do for you?"

"There is one thing." I untied Gor's skull from my belt by touch and passed it between the bars. "Take this to the burial place and leave it in the corner where the oldest graves reside."

"Should I stay there and wait?"

"No. You would probably be killed. My message will be understood. Go now, before a guard comes."

I heard his feet withdraw across the sand of the alley behind the jailhouse. Turning from the window, I realized the old man had ceased to mumble. He was awake.

"Are you a djinn?" he asked in a fearful voice through the darkness.

His mind must have been half-addled with drink and fever. I considered his question.

"I am half-djinn, or so I have been told."

"Are you going to kill me, too?"

Again, I considered. "Not tonight."

At that he fell silent, and soon his fevered mumbling resumed. He was ill with some disease. This did not worry me. My body is uncommonly resistant to sickness, another gift from my unknown father.

Chapter 12

n the morning the guards found the corpse and took it away. Trievos came and questioned me. His manner was grave, and I noticed that he took care to stay at least two paces from me at all times. I did not intend to kill him, but how could he know this? I told him the truth, that the other man had tried to strangle me in my sleep, and that I had torn out his throat with my teeth. What could he say? The old man was incoherent and could neither confirm nor deny my account.

"The mayor wishes to question you," he said. I did not like the extra emphasis he placed on the word *question*.

When I stepped out of the cell into the morning light, I realized the entire front of my tunic was matted with dried blood. The guards recoiled from me instinctively. For a moment I thought it was because they saw my true face, but no, my mask of glamour was still intact. I turned away from them and renewed it with a muttered word and a gesture, just to be certain.

The absence of the ghoul's skull at my belt elicited no comment from them. Either they did not notice it was gone, or simply did not care what became of it. They marched me across a dusty plaza toward an official-looking building of two levels that I took to be the town meeting hall. Trievos followed close behind me. I was taken through a side entrance and down a long corridor to a windowless room at the rear of the building.

When I saw how the room was decorated, my heart fell. There were instruments of torture hanging from the walls and arrayed on tables. An iron charcoal brazier glowed red. In it rested a pair of identical iron pokers.

They wasted no time, but stripped me naked and bound me to an upright rack by the wrists, neck, waist, and ankles. Fortunately, the glamour that conceals my true face also hides my castration. To their eyes my sexual organs were intact, and uncommonly handsome. The spell is a simple one but subtle, for it does not conceal injuries that occur to my body while it is in place, but only the mutilations that were done before it was applied. It is designed this way to make its detection more difficult.

My captors left me without speaking so much as a word. For an hour or more I contemplated the instruments of torture by lamplight. Some of them I recognized all too well. The iron hooks for forcing open the mouth, that do so much damage to the teeth. The heated pokers for searing the skin. The knives to slash and slice the flesh. Others were unfamiliar to me, and I entertained myself by imagining how they were used. This was the intention of those who had placed me here. They wanted to frighten me into babbling before I was even hurt.

A burly man who wore a long brown leather apron that covered his chest and thighs, and a leather hood over the upper part of his face that concealed everything but his eyes and mouth, entered and made himself busy stirring the charcoal in the brazier, so that a cloud of sparks flew up and it glowed a brighter orange. From the embers he withdrew one of the pair of iron pokers and examined its glowing point. He did not look at me or speak.

After a time another man entered. He had the air of someone with many things to do and not enough time in the day to do them. His robes were conservative in cut but of the highest quality. A tall man, he stood almost a full head above the hooded torturer. His lips were sensual, his nose long and thin, but the feature that stood out the most was his ears. He was not wearing a headscarf, and his ears were the largest I have ever seen. They covered half the sides of his head, their lobes drooping down like half-filled wine sacks. He stared around at the instruments of pain with an expression of distaste, then turned to me.

"Answer my questions swiftly and truthfully, and I promise you, we will not need to resort to these devices."

"Are you Hafiz ibd Ahmad, the mayor of this town?"

"I am. And you are the one who calls himself Abdul Alhazred."

"That is my name."

"Why have you come to Jubbah?"

"Being a man of means and leisure, it amuses me at times to travel and see distant places."

"Do you always travel with a mercenary?"

"The roads are dangerous."

"Is that why you travel with a young girl who dresses like a man? Or is her function merely to warm your bed?"

This surprised me. I wondered how he had learned that Martala was female. She had not revealed herself outside of Thalmus's house.

"My young nephew is of slight build, I grant you, but I would scarcely call him a girl."

"What do you seek in Jubbah?"

"I confess, I am puzzled by the thrust of your questions. I imagined you would ask me about the events in the alehouse, or about the incident in my cell."

"Those matters hold no interest for me."

While we talked, a man entered the room and stood behind him in the shadows, silently listening and watching. When at last he stepped into the lamplight, I saw that it was Fayez ibn-Hakim. There was no malice in his keen eyes as he regarded my predicament, and no pity, only a cold calculation.

"This one will not talk unless he is put to the torture," the mayor said.

"I suspect he will not talk even then, but we must make the experiment."

I screamed each time it was applied.

"Why waste time asking me questions to which you already know the answers?" I demanded. It annoyed me that I had not guessed Fayez might be in collusion with the leaders of Jubbah.

"Very well, we will speak honestly," Fayez said. "We know you came here to obtain the red stone. We know you are an agent for a man of wealth and power in Damascus. Naturally we have our suspicions as to who that man may be. I want you to name him."

"I came here to enjoy the wildflowers, and to do a little climbing on the mountain."

He smiled. "How did you enjoy your last climbing expedition?"

"Someone shot me with an arrow."

"The mountain can be dangerous for the unwary. Roving bandits conceal themselves among its ridges, and it is so easy to lose your way."

"It was not a total waste of time. We discovered some fascinating rock carvings."

"Did they fascinate you? I have found the mountain to be covered with them, and none of them conveys information of any value."

"Perhaps you have looked in the wrong places."

His eyes narrowed with impatience. "No, we have looked in every place, and I tell you, Alhazred, there is nothing on the mountain that will assist your quest. If it was there I would know of it."

"Then why do you still search the mountain?"

"This banter of words is a waste of time," the mayor said. He looked at the torturer. "Apply the iron."

The masked man took a poker from the glowing bed of coals in the brazier and held its red tip near my face, turning it this way and that.

"When you tell me who has employed you to locate the stone, the pain will stop," Hafiz said.

The iron was pressed against my body numerous times, beginning with my feet and moving upward over my limbs and torso. I screamed each time it was applied.

81

When it became too cold to sear my flesh, it was replaced in the brazier and the other identical to it was taken from the charcoal, so that I had no time to recover myself from the pain.

The burn marks showed through the veil of magic that concealed my mutilations. The air of the chamber, already acrid with the smoke of the charcoal, became thick with the stench of burnt flesh.

"As entertaining as this spectacle is, I cannot waste any more of my time here," Fayez told the mayor.

"Do you think I enjoy this foul work? It is for your benefit that I do this, not mine."

"You have been well paid for your assistance."

"Not well enough, I think. That fool Trievos is beginning to wonder why we are so often together."

"Are you certain his compliance cannot be bought?"

"He is a man of honor, may he be cursed for it. If he knew you were paying me to subvert the law, he would expose me to the council and the mullahs."

This was interesting information. If the magistrate was honest, it might be possible at some future juncture to enlist his aid.

"Be warned; should Trievos become an obstruction to my purposes, I may have to kill him."

"Do not tell me that," Hafiz said in annoyance. "It is not something I need to know."

"You hug your ignorance like a cloak," Fayez said with contempt.

"I care nothing for your opinion, only for your gold. With it I shall buy a house and lands in Alexandria or some other civilized city, where I will live out my days in contentment, far from this hated oasis."

"Keep your foolish dreams to yourself," Fayez told him. "You are a tool to be used, and it disgusts me to use you. This man you torture is twice the man you are."

"Many thanks for the compliment," I muttered through dry lips.

Fayez glanced at me, and laughed. "You have spirit, Alhazred. Know this, I have no hatred against you, but I have been assigned a task and I cannot allow you to obstruct me. I regret the necessity of killing you."

"What is this talk of killing?" Hafiz said in alarm. "You mentioned nothing about a killing when you drew me into your schemes."

"Be a man," Fayez said. "We cannot allow him to go free, to bear witness against us. He knows he must die, just as you should know it."

The mayor shook his head so that his earlobes jiggled like the breasts of a dancer. "I am not a murderer."

"No, you are much less. But do not be concerned. When the time comes, all you need do is turn your eyes away."

Fayez left the chamber. The mayor continued to demand the name of my patron but his mind was distracted by his conversation with Fayez, and the torture did not last as long as before. Even so, it was afternoon before he ceased.

"Enough for today," he told the torturer. "Return him to the cell. Give him neither food nor water."

He turned to me, and I thought that I perceived a shadow of guilt in his eyes, or perhaps it was shame. But I may be giving him more credit than he deserved. It may only have been disgust.

"Tomorrow we will begin again, and we will not be so gentle. There is no escape for you, Alhazred. Answer my questions, and I promise that your pain will end and your manner of death will be easy. If you continue to defy me, what you have suffered today will seem like the caress of a lover."

I felt the urge to mock him but held my tongue. He was not a talented torturer. He lacked the necessary imagination to inspire terror in his victims. For what he had done, I would kill him, unless he killed me first.

Chapter 13

The guards gave me back my clothing and allowed me to dress myself. Then they escorted me across the plaza to the jail and locked me inside. The old man still lay shivering on his sleeping mat, talking to whatever came to him in his fever dreams. The water pitcher had been removed. No food was brought. I thought it unfair that the old man should suffer my punishment, but he was not in a state of health to care. Shortly after the fall of night he took one final inhalation of breath and released it slowly. By the time it ceased to rattle in his throat he was dead.

I welcomed the silence. Apart from an occasional burst of drunken laughter or the bark of a dog, the night was still. My body ached from dozens of burns. Whenever I moved, my blood-encrusted tunic rubbed or pressed against one or more red marks seared into my skin, sending a flash of pain along my nerves. They would leave scars, of that there was no doubt, but I cared little for the appearance of my body. I was more concerned about the possibility of the burns becoming infected. Fortunately, I had a natural resistance to infection.

"Alhazred?" a voice whispered through the bars of the window.

"Bakka?" I stood, trying to ignore the complaints from all parts of my skin, and went to the window. It was too dark to see more than the outline of the ghoul's head against the stars.

"I got your message." He passed something through the bars, and I realized as I took it that it was Gor's skull.

"I hope you did not harm my messenger."

He laughed. "The fool hid himself at the edge of the burial ground and tried to see us. We came and took the skull, and he was none the wiser."

"Is he unharmed?"

"He is healthy enough. The last I saw of him he was making his way back toward Jubbah."

"I need to escape from this place. They plan to kill me."

I told him about the alliance between the mayor of the town and the agent of Marwan ibn al-Hakam. Ghouls were no strangers to plots and intrigues. Their clans were at constant war with each other. He understood immediately the trap that had been laid for me and my companions long before we came to Jubbah.

"You were expected, or at least anticipated."

"So it appears."

"You cannot remain inside the walls of the town."

"No. Trievos will be sent to look for me."

"You can stay with us in our warren."

"That is generous, but I cannot hide myself in a hole in the earth. I came to Jubbah for a purpose, and I must pursue it."

"What would you do?"

I had already considered the matter, but I thought for several minutes without speaking.

"I want you to take me up on the mountain to where the witch has been seen at twilight. I need to talk with her."

He sucked air through his bared teeth.

"That is a very bad idea, Alhazred. Those who seek out the witch never return from the mountain."

"Even so, I can think of no other course that lies open for me."

"Very well, it shall be as you ask."

"First I need to go back to the house of Thalmus for clean clothing and weapons. How do you plan to free me from this prison?"

"Your freedom has been in the making since I received your friend's skull and learned of your imprisonment."

"These iron bars are stout," I said, gripping them doubtfully in my fists. "The door is thick and bound with plates of iron. It would take a siege engine to break these walls."

Bakka chuckled.

"You are not thinking like a ghoul, Alhazred. You have dwelt at Damascus for too long."

A scratching noise came behind me from the floor. I thought it was a rat, but it grew louder. I heard the sifting of sand and the crumbling of packed clay.

"My clan has tunnels under every part of Jubbah. They are very old. They were dug long before the time of my father's father. I suppose they were dug so that should the supply of corpses in the burial ground be insufficient, it would be possible to take food from the streets and houses of the town. It was a trifling labor to extend one of these tunnels under your prison. As you know, ghouls are excellent at digging the earth."

He raised his hand and wiggled his fingers. I saw starlight reflected in the polished surface of his black claws.

"Come with me," a ghoul's voice whispered from the center of the cell near the floor.

I left the window and approached cautiously, feeling the floor with my fingers as I went. I felt the ragged edge of a hole and the warm skin of a ghoul.

"Follow," the ghoul said.

Slipping my legs into the hole, I dropped to the bottom and followed the sound of his progress. We crawled for no great distance and climbed up into a silent building that was as dark as my cell. Bakka was already there.

"I need to return to the house of the sage Thalmus to get clean clothing and weapons, and to talk to my companions."

"We will go quickly. We must leave the village before dawn."

"What about the hole in the jail cell?"

Several ghouls who were in the room chuckled.

"By the time you leave Jubbah, there will be no hole, only a spot of disturbed earth on the floor of the cell."

I grinned in the darkness. To Fayez and the mayor, it would be as though I had vanished like smoke in the air.

Leaving his fellow ghouls to fill the tunnel, Bakka went with me to the house of Thalmus.

"I will wait on the street," he said uneasily. "When you are ready, come to me and I will take you to the mountain."

I understood. Ghouls avoid the places of men. There is too much light, too many dogs, too many chances of discovery. It had taken courage for Bakka and his clan-mates to enter the walls of Jubbah.

The wall of the house would not prove a difficult climb, although the top was probably studded with broken glass and pot shards. Before climbing it, I softly called Altrus by name, on the chance that he was waiting outside the house.

"Alhazred, wait by the gate, I will open it," he called back.

He came to the gate. I heard the rattle of the latch. Bakka melted back into the darkness. The gate opened.

"We can't stay in this house," I whispered as I went past him. "They are sure to come for us here."

"Where are we to go?" he asked behind me.

I entered the house as silently as I could and held the door for him.

"We must be apart for a time. I am going with the ghouls into the mountain to see what I can learn from a witch who is said to dwell on its summit. I want you to take the girl and go outside the walls to live among the Bedouin until I return."

"I don't like this plan," he muttered. "It could get you killed."

The house was silent. I went up the stairs to the room Thalmus had given me. Martala lay in bed. I heard her regular breaths and thought she was asleep, but when I got near she threw back the sheet and slid out of bed. I reached out my hand to touch her. She was already dressed.

"It's me," I whispered.

"I know."

This surprised me. I could see almost nothing in the murk. "How did you know?"

She suppressed a giggle. "By your smell, of course."

I slid my hand over the crusted front of my tunic, amazed that she could smell anything beneath the pervasive stench of dried blood. It was perhaps time for me to take a bath. Unfortunately the opportunity did not present itself.

I had not brought with me a second tunic, but I carried in my travel bag a white cotton thawb of the same kind that she and Altrus wore. As I threw off my filthy clothing and robed myself in clean garments, I told her what had transpired since our last meeting. She made no objection when I said that she must leave the house and go with Altrus outside the walls of the town.

"I have news for you," she said when I ceased to speak. "Today I saw our host talking with the daughter of Fayez, if indeed she is his daughter, which I very much doubt."

"It is as I feared. Thalmus has been bribed to act in the service of Fayez, just as has the major of Jubbah. I suspected as much when his servant tried to kill me, and the map he gave me supported my suspicions. It was not faulty but deliberately misdrawn so that we would become lost on the mountain, and wander where Fayez and his mercenaries lay in wait for us."

"I will kill the old man," Altrus said.

For a moment I entertained the thought.

"No. It was my decision that caused us to sleep under his roof. The responsibility is mine."

Digging through my travel pack, I drew out the dagger that I had placed there before leaving Damascus. Altrus brought me a sword that he had found somewhere in the house. He must have noticed it during the day and marked its location in his memory. Whether it belonged to the old man or one of his servants, I did not ask. It was an inferior blade but better than nothing.

I left them to continue their preparations to depart the

house and made my way down the hall to the bedroom of the old man. The hall was silent as a tomb, the servants deep in slumber. To my surprise, the old man's door was not bolted. It opened noiselessly. My eyes were fully adapted to the night. I was able to see the faint outline of furniture and a bed. From it I heard the sound of soft breathing.

Drawing my dagger, I approached the side of the bed and leaned over it.

"Do you intend to kill me?" Thalmus asked quietly. There was no fear in his voice, only a leaden note of fatality.

I hesitated only for an instant.

"Yes," I said.

He released a slow breath.

"I don't blame you for it. I've lived a long life, and most of it has been lived in the fear of other men. I fled from Damascus to this oasis in fear, and remained here in exile out of fear. I agreed to order Happisus to murder you because I was afraid to refuse. But tonight, I am not afraid. Do what you must."

Pressing my palm over his mouth, I thrust the point of my dagger into his breast between his ribs, just below his heart. I heard the blade cut the individual threads of his nightshirt as it slid in. He twitched and struggled for a few moments, then relaxed as the life flowed from his body.

My companions were ready for me when I emerged from the old man's chamber and closed the door. They said nothing about what I had just done. I knew that Altrus approved of my action. If the girl disapproved, she chose not to speak. The three of us went softly down the stairs and out the front door of the house. We stopped just inside the iron gate.

"Now I will leave you," I told them. "Get the camels. Take them outside the walls. The Bedouin will conceal you among them if you pay them well. Dress as they dress and remain invisible, but continue to watch the doings of Fayez and his mercenaries. I will return as soon as I have spoken with the witch and learned what I can learn from her."

Martala stepped close in the dark and laid her hand on my chest.

"Take care, Alhazred. You know you are as helpless as a little child when we are not with you."

"So that's what you think of me," I said, smiling in spite of myself.

"You act recklessly and fail to guard your back," Altrus said.

"I remind the two of you that before we met, I survived naked and alone in the Empty Space."

This meant nothing to them. In so many ways they were the children. But I was touched by their concern.

We left the house together with our hands over our weapons in their sheaths so that they would not strike our legs as we moved. I saw the shadow of Bakka lurking across the street. Martala and Altrus did not see him.

"Go now; get the camels. Their boarding is paid in advance for another week. Take them among the Bedouin. I must go another way."

They spoke not a word but stole away down the dark street.

I went to the ghoul.

"Guide me to the witch."

Chapter 14

I was not sure we would have enough of the night left to reach Salamagoogah. Ghouls cannot bear the daylight. It blinds them and burns their skin. But they can move with great rapidity when they have a need to do so, and they are tireless. It was not long before I was gasping for breath as I followed Bakka out of the town and across the plain toward Jabal Umm Sanman.

He ascended the mountain with sure steps. The way must have been well known to him, though why that should be was a puzzle. I could not imagine any use the mountain would be to ghouls.

As we approached the flat but irregular summit, he stopped and pointed ahead at two upthrusting ridges.

"That is where the witch has been seen, crossing those ridges at twilight. Her den must be somewhere nearby. Now I will leave you."

I glanced at the eastern sky with concern. Already it was becoming light.

"Can you get back to your warren before sunrise?"

"No. But I know a deep place where I can sleep and wait for night. I am sorry that I cannot stand beside you when you face the witch."

"You have done more than hospitality required," I assured him. "Your clan behaved with honor."

This formal declaration pleased him, as I knew it would. He left me with a hearty slap between the shoulder blades and a chuckling laugh. In a moment he merged with the shadows.

The witch was said by the ghouls to move about on the mountain in the twilight. If this was true, she should emerge soon from her hiding place, for sunrise was not many minutes distant. I found a hollow that was not far removed from the ridges and crouched on my heels to wait.

The sun was still below the horizon, but the first light began to transform the shadows into grey shapes. There were masses of rock everywhere along with tumbled boulders as large as houses.

Something moved in a narrow cleft between two buttresses of rock, a shadow against the shadowy interior. A figure slowly emerged. It was a woman cloaked from head to foot in black, with a black veil across her face. Not even her eyes were visible, but her fingers gripping the hem of her cloak beneath her chin looked like white worms in the greyness.

She made her way along the ridges Bakka had indicated and down the slope. I saw that she carried an empty waterskin. Her way of moving was uncanny. She almost appeared to drift from the cover of one boulder to the next, never exposing herself fully to observation. I realized it was some kind of spell to conceal her movements that was not wholly effective, or at least, not on me. She must be making her way to a watering place amid the rocks—probably a hidden pool of water fed by a bubbling spring.

Instead of following her, I allowed her to work her cautious way beyond my sight. Then I hurried to the cleft from which she had emerged and pressed my body sideways into it. The opening was tall but narrow. I had to shift Gor's skull on my belt to fit through.

A passage that did not appear to have been cut by men led downward. I soon left the light behind me. My progress was slow because I was compelled to feel for each step before taking it lest I step off the edge of a precipice. I wondered if the witch could see in the dark.

The question was answered when I emerged into a cavern high enough for me to stand without fear of banging my head. A stone oil lamp burned on a natural ledge, giving me a good view of what the cavern contained. It was furnished as a living space. On one side was a felt mattress covered with two wool blankets. On the other stood a small wooden table and chair, and a finely made wooden cabinet. I tried to open the door of the cabinet but found it locked. Its top surface was cluttered with wooden bowls and cups. An iron cauldron hung from a tripod over a hearth in the center of the floor. I looked up and saw the blackened opening of a fissure that acted as a natural chimney. There was a shelf of books, all of them worm-eaten and moldering.

I wondered how the witch had managed to get such furniture up the side of the mountain undetected. None of it was too large to be carried by one person, although the cabinet must have been an awkward burden. It would have been necessary to take apart the table and chair in order to get them through the narrow fissure, but it was not impossible to believe that the witch had put them back together. Perhaps she had been raiding the camps of the caravans that came to the oasis for her furnishings.

The cavern might almost have been homelike were it not for a pervasive odor that hung in the air. It was a mixture of grease and smoke and putrefaction. I curled my upper lip in disgust. The scent of decay itself holds no horror for me, but this was a smell that has worked its way into the very rock walls over a span of centuries. And there was something else. At the margin of the lamp glow I saw bones. They were human and had been gnawed clean of all traces of flesh.

I went to the still-warm hearth and looked inside the iron pot. It was filled with a kind of soup. It was not scalding hot—the fire had died down to embers hours ago. Curiosity got the better of me. I pulled my sleeve back to my elbow, reached into the pot, and felt around. I drew out several finger joints with the cooked flesh still clinging to the bones, and a thumb that was intact.

The witch and I share something in common, I thought, and had to resist the urge to laugh in self-mockery. How many years had she lived here alone, hidden from the world, preying on unwary men who climbed the mountain or wandered along on the plain? It was not uncommon for witches to dwell apart. They were driven out of towns and villages. Their neighbors shunned them, and their very families turned their backs upon them. I felt a strange sense of kinship with this woman. I, too, had been accused of necromancy and driven from my home in Yemen.

I studied her books. Some were in Greek, several in Hebrew, the rest in an Arabic script. They all concerned magic in one form or another. Most witches were illiterate. This one appeared to be something of a scholar.

I dragged the solitary wooden chair from under the table and turned it so that it faced the entrance of the cavern, then sat in it with my arms folded across my chest to wait.

She returned in a little more than an hour. When she entered, she saw me immediately, but did not react as I expected. She merely nodded to me behind her obscuring veil and hung her filled waterskin up on an iron spike by its leather strap.

"I am Abdul Alhazred, and I have come here to speak with you, Salamagoogah, about the red stone of Jubbah."

"You were on the mountain," she said as she crouched before the hearth and stirred the ashes to expose a glowing ember. This she fanned and blew into a brightness until it sprang into flame and caught the kindling she slid under the hanging pot.

"That's right. I was searching for the stone."

"A woman tried to kill you with a bow." Her voice was surprisingly mellow. I had expected it to crack with age.

"Its force was spent, and its point struck my rib."

She stood up and drew off her headdress and veil, shaking loose her long black hair. She was one of the most beautiful women I have ever seen. Her complexion was olive but unblemished, her lips full and red, her eyes a deep green.

She wore no cosmetics, but the thickness of her eyebrows and the length of her eyelashes gave the illusion that she was painted with kohl. I judged her age to be twenty-five, but could not have sworn to it. She had the kind of timeless face that looks the same from its twenties to its forties. The bridge of her nose was as straight as any Greek's.

"Will you take supper with me?" She indicated the cauldron.

"I would be honored to share your evening meal."

She gestured to the bones on the floor of the cavern. "Even knowing the source of my meat?"

I shrugged. "Meat is meat."

Her eyes wandered to my belt. "Is that the skull of a ghoul?"

I nodded.

"A strange ornament for a man of obvious breeding and education."

Spreading my arms, I looked around the cavern.

"I might say the same. A strange home for a woman of such obvious attainments."

She stirred the iron cauldron with a wooden spoon, and used the end of its handle to brush a strand of hair from over her eye.

"Once I lived among men. I grew weary of their ceaseless chatter."

I had been studying the outline of her body, but had discovered no weapon. If she wore a dagger, it was well concealed.

"Pursuit of the arcane arts requires silence and solitude."

She glanced at me. "You speak as one who knows the meaning of his words."

"I have some knowledge of necromancy."

"A noble art," she said. "Not my primary study, but a noble art."

We said little as we waited for the crackling fire to heat the cauldron. When steam rose from the surface of the soup, she went to her cabinet and took two wooden bowls and two small wooden spoons from its top. She filled my bowl with a copper ladle and handed it to me along with a spoon. I crouched on my heels beside the fire, as she did.

"Do you not know the Greek fable of Circe?" she asked.

"You are not Circe," I said with a smile, "and I am not Odysseus."

"You are a brave man to come here, Alhazred. I doubt there is another man in Jubbah who would have done it."

"There is one, at least," I said, thinking of Altrus.

"Don't you know what they say about me? That I hold communion with djinn? That I am ten thousand years old? That I come from Babylon? That I waylay and murder men for my food?"

"Is any of that true?"

"All of it is true."

I tasted the soup. It was quite good. I began to eat it with enthusiasm.

"Does it not horrify you to know what is in your soup?"

"If you mean to horrify me, you'll have to do better than that."

We made inconsequential table conversation as we ate. I discovered that she was a woman of refinement and manners. At some period in her past she must have lived in a royal court, for there was no other way to acquire her social attainments. Her knowledge of literature and history was more extensive than my own.

When we set our empty bowls aside, she went to her bed and sat on one end of it, beckoning for me to sit on the other end.

Be wary. She is trying to seduce you, Alhazred, Sashi said in my mind. Her face drifted before my inner sight, and wore an expression of disapproval.

If she tries that, she will be disappointed, I thought back to the djinn.

"Now, Alhazred the necromancer, tell me what has brought you to this remote oasis."

"I have been sent to find the red stone of Jubbah, and to carry it back with me to Damascus."

She laughed with obvious delight, and her laughter was musical. "I cannot number the men who, over the centuries, have come to Jubbah to search for the red stone, and all of them were disappointed."

"This I can well believe, for I have found nothing at Jubbah that would indicate the resting place of the stone, or even if it still survives."

"Oh, it survives. Time has no dominion over such things."

"Do you know where it is?"

She met my eyes more seriously. "No. But I know where you may find a rock carving bearing a map that shows its place of concealment."

"Was it deliberately hidden?"

She nodded. "As the fame of the red stone spread, the people they call the Thamud carried it from Persia into Arabia, and then from the south of Arabia into these northern lands to keep it safe, but men still pursued it, so they devised a place of concealment for the stone. There it has rested undisturbed for centuries."

"The stone survived its caretakers," I murmured.

"Not entirely," she said. "There are still Thamud dwelling in the caverns beneath this mountain."

"Can you take me to them?"

"It would be futile. They have degenerated through incestuous breeding over their many generations beneath the earth, and are scarce above the level of beasts. If they ever possessed knowledge of value, they possess it no longer."

"It is strange that a tribe would uproot itself from its home time after time, merely to protect a piece of rock."

"The stone has great power," she said, and her green eyes glistened as she spoke. "It confers invincibility on the man who possesses it. He becomes unconquerable in war."

"If this stone is so powerful, and you know of a map to its hiding place, why have you not taken possession of it yourself?"

Her expression darkened.

"The stone gives power only to men. Any woman who

touches it dies. Were this not so, I would long ago have made it mine. Besides—" She hesitated.

"Yes? What were you about to tell me?"

"It is nothing, a fable to frighten fools."

"Even so, I would like to hear it."

"They say the stone has a protective spirit that will kill anyone who tries to remove it from its resting place."

"What is the nature of this spirit? Is it a djinn?"

"No, not a djinn. Something else. The legend is not explicit as to its nature."

This information I mulled over in my mind. It was not uncommon for precious objects to have undead guardians set over them.

"I will be wary of this spirit. Now tell me how to find the map to the hiding place of the stone."

"This I will do on one condition. Will you pledge to honour my terms?"

"How can I do that before I know them?"

"You must. Tell me you will do what I require, or I will not reveal the location of the rock carvings that speak of the stone."

"What is to prevent me from forcing the information from your lips," I said quietly.

She laughed, this time softly, and her eyes were bright. "It would be interesting to watch you attempt it. But truly, Alhazred, it is not necessary. All I require from you is a trifling service."

"Very well, I agree to fulfill your terms."

"Good. It is only this—I want you to bring the red stone back to me here, on this mountain, so that I may look upon it before you carry it away."

"You only wish to gaze upon it?"

"What more could I do? If I touch it, the stone will kill me. I only wish to gaze upon this famed stone, over which so much has been written, and so much blood has been spilled."

I did not trust her. It was obvious she had some deceptive motive in asking me to bring her the stone. She meant to betray me, of that I had no doubt. This seemed fair enough, for I had every intention of betraying her.

"The rock carving that reveals the resting place of the stone has never been found, for one very good reason," she said. "It is not on Jabal Umm Sanman. The carving is located on the mountain called Ghouwtah, which is about fourteen miles eastward from the town of Jubbah."

My heart leapt up with excitement at this information. I felt I was finally on the trail of the stone, after so many false leads and dead ends.

Chapter 15

Once again we were on our gently rocking camels, but this time we rode east. The flatness of the plain coupled with its lack of sand made the terrain dreamlike. Heat shimmered on the horizon like lakes of mercury, and dust devils danced around the rocks. Here and there were patches of green, and even the brighter colors of wildflowers. The water of the rains that had fallen shortly before our arrival still lay close beneath the surface. To my judgment the plain appeared more of a garden than a desert, but I measured all deserts against the harsh rule of the Empty Space.

It was Altrus who first noticed the cloud of dust behind us. Whatever made the dust was too distant to be seen through the sliding silver bands of heat, but he expressed no doubt as to its source.

"Camels," he said in a tone of disgust.

"How many?" I asked.

"At least six or seven, probably more."

"It could be mere chance," Martala suggested.

We withheld our judgment.

My own thought was that Fayez must have had a spy among the Bedouin who saw us depart the oasis and ran to inform him of the event. They could not know where we were going, so they had probably followed with the intention of killing us all. If so, Fayez would bring all his men.

"We must keep a rapid pace," I said. "We do not want to fall within bowshot."

"At least this time we have a bow of our own," Martala said.

She wore across her back a strung bow of black lacquered wood that she had purchased from the tribesmen among whom she and Altrus had concealed the camels. Beside it hung a quiver of leather that held about two dozen hunting arrows. The girl was an excellent marksman with the bow. If nothing else, it would keep our pursuers at a respectful distance.

The plain played with our expectation. Ghouwtah was a smaller mountain than Jabal Umm Sanman. For many hours it appeared to maintain the same distance. Then, of a sudden, it loomed before us. It was late afternoon. The ride to the mountain had taken most of the day.

"What now?" Martala asked aloud as we surveyed the unpromising slope covered with loose rock that reared before us.

"We find the rock carvings the witch spoke about," I said.

"They could be anywhere," Altrus said.

"All the more reason not to delay our search."

We began to ride around the mountain in a sunwise circle. After a time we came upon a faint track that led up the slope at a gentle angle. It was wide enough for a camel. It did not look as though any foot, human or beast, had trodden it for centuries.

As we sat contemplating it, Altrus said, "It is a defensible position. If nothing else, the elevation will give us a better vantage from which to watch for those who follow us."

He was a seasoned mercenary who wanted us to secure the high ground, should it come to a battle. I did not question his judgment. We followed the path upward, me in the lead and the girl at the end. It wound and twisted around outcroppings of stone and through gorges that looked as though they had been carved in some distant past age by torrents of floodwater. Everything had an ancient look to it. The stones of the mountain itself were weathered and old.

This was a place where the passage of time was measured, not in days, but in millennia.

When we were at the elevation of the summit, or near to it, the way opened into a small canyon with sheer walls of no great height. Several cairns of stones, obviously erected by men, stood on its floor, and there was another more refined construction of neatly fitted stones that looked like a sacrificial altar.

On one of the canyon walls, flatter and less fissured than the rest, a set of carvings had been deeply incised. Even so, the rock face was so weathered, it was difficult to distinguish some of the symbols. I dismounted and went closer to study them.

There were the usual depictions of men and camels, some horses, what looked like goats, and wagons. The carvings showed a caravan crossing the desert. In one wagon that was incised with special care there rested a trunk. From the trunk radiated rays like sunbeams.

"It looks like a depiction of the Ark of the Hebrews." I had seen similar drawings in books in King Huban's library at Yemen.

A little further along there was a scene of warfare. A king or a general stood in a chariot holding aloft a globe with rays radiating from it. Around him men fought with clubs and swords. Their bodies lay scattered across the field of battle, along with horses and war dogs.

This carving was followed by the unmistakable outline of Jabal Umm Sanman. Next to it was another scene I recognized. It was the cleft between the upthrust natural buttresses of stone that formed the entrance to Salamagoogah's cave. Four men were entering the cleft, carrying the trunk between them suspended from leather straps. From it radiated beams of light. Behind them, six other men bore on their shoulders the corpse of a man with his hands folded stiffly over his chest. Something hovered in the air over them. It was not a bird or a bat, but it had leathern wings of a kind, and something that resembled a hawk's talons on its feet.

Other men raised their arms and cowered away in fear or awe from the flying creature.

The final scene was near the bottom of the slab of rock, and was larger and more elaborate than the other carvings. It depicted a domed hall or tomb. The corpse lay atop an oblong stone that was elevated high above the floor on a kind of pyramid with steps cut into its sloping sides. A shining globe meant to represent the red stone rested on its chest between its hands. Men knelt on either side of the pyramid and bowed their heads and extended their arms upward toward the corpse in postures of worship.

Anger boiled within my breast. For a moment I could not speak because of it, but I soon brought myself under control.

"The witch betrayed me. She sent me to my death. She must have known that Fayez and his mercenaries would follow me. The stone is under Jabal Umm Sanman."

"She may not know the stone is there," Martala said.

I pointed at the carving that showed the cleft between the rocks. "This is where she dwells. How could she not be aware that the stone is hidden beneath her lair?"

"What is that?" Altrus asked, pointing at the winged creature.

"A demon of some kind. I do not recognize its type."

"I recognize this," the girl said, touching a symbol carved above the corpse in the final scene. "But I can't remember where I've seen it."

For the first time, I studied it with attention. My anger had caused me to overlook it. The symbol was a circle with a cross above it.

"That is one of the symbols for the planet Mars in astrology, or for iron in alchemy," I told her. "You must have seen it in the books in my library."

"What does its presence here mean?"

I tried to think, but my mind was on the assassins who even now rode across the plain toward us, and on the betrayal of the witch. It was true that I had intended to betray her, but it galled me that she had betrayed me first.

"I don't know."

Altrus looked at the sky, then at our camels. "The day is late. We could not reach Jubbah before darkness fell. We must decide whether to make our stand here, or to flee away from Ghouwtah under the veil of night. We must decide soon, or Fayez will have the way down from this cursed mountain blocked."

Fayez would see us when we left the mountain, for it would still be daylight, and we dared not wait for darkness before we left or he would have reached us. I thought about fleeing across the darkening plain ahead of his men, but did not like the prospect. There was nowhere to go except back to Jubbah. Whichever way we rode in the light, he would know it was a trick, and that we must turn our mounts to the oasis in the end, and he would position himself so that he was waiting to ambush us.

"We will stay the night here. The entrance to this canyon is narrow and easy to defend. With luck, we may be able to kill enough of his men to make him think twice about confronting us."

I could see by his expression that Altrus did not entirely agree with my decision, but he held his tongue. This was just as well. I was in a foul mood. I wanted to tighten my fingers around the neck of the witch, and gritted my teeth together whenever I thought of her. I wondered if she, too, was in league with Fayez. It seemed he had bribed the entire population of the oasis.

"Good," Martala said with satisfaction. She unslung the bow from her shoulders. "I've been aching to use this."

"You're a bloodthirsty little Egyptian," Altrus said with a grin.

"I'm not a sheep to be led to the slaughter, if that's what you mean."

"There's nothing sheep-like about you, girl."

"When they climb the path, they won't know what lies above. We may be able to surprise them," I said.

Martala notched an arrow to her bow and drew it in practice.

"If I can kill Fayez, the rest will lose interest."

"At least one of them has a bow," I reminded her. "Probably more than one."

We ate a little of our dried food and drank some water after caring for our camels and staking them in a sheltered place. Then we took our positions and watched down the path that led to the canyon entrance, listening for voices or the grunts of camels. The afternoon light grayed into twilight.

There was little chance our pursuers could come at us from any other direction. Fayez almost certainly was unfamiliar with the mountain, and we had seen only one way up Ghouwtah. In any event the footprints of our beasts lead directly to it. No, they would come with caution, but this was surely the way they would come.

Martala touched my arm. Through the gathering gloom I saw a man crouching behind a rock some distance down the slope of the path. He had his dagger drawn and wore a grim expression. Fayez had sent him ahead to test the way. All the greater misfortune for him.

I nodded to the girl. She grinned with delight, so that I saw the flash of her white teeth through the gloom, and drew the fletching of an arrow against her cheek. The thrum of the bowstring seemed loud in the silence. The man gurgled with an arrow through his neck, and slowly tumbled from behind the rock into the middle of the path.

"Alhazred, we know you are up there," Fayez called out. "You have nowhere to run. Surrender to us and we will spare your lives."

"As you spared the life of Happisus?" I called back.

"The Egyptian was a fool. He acted in haste and paid the price for his inability to follow orders."

For a minute I let the silence lengthen between us.

"I've considered your offer, but it does not please me. Instead, I think we will kill you all one by one as you struggle up this steepness of the path."

"That is not the way it will be, my friend. I beg you to reconsider."

"No."

"That is unfortunate, for now I must kill you."

Chapter 16

man's intention, even when so confidently expressed, does not always find fulfillment. The three of us set about ensuring that Fayez would be disappointed.

Martala climbed to the top of one of the thrusting rocks that bordered the entrance to the canyon. From her seat she had a commanding view of the ascending path, which twisted between the boulders like a serpent. There was little cover on the path. Anyone ascending it would be exposed, at least for several seconds. Altrus and I positioned ourselves on opposite sides of the entrance, so that any of Fayez's mercenaries who managed to escape the girl's arrows would meet our swords.

My concerns were twofold. I worried that Fayez would choose to simply wait us out until we were dying from thirst. This he could do by guarding the path and sending one of his men back to Jubbah for fresh water. Eventually our water would be exhausted. My other worry was that Fayez would somehow find a way up the rocks behind us. We would be easy targets for archers if they managed to get to the rim of the canyon wall. The walls of the canyon did not appear easy to climb, but I could not know the condition of the outer slopes.

To probe our defences, Fayez sent another of his less prudent mercenaries running up the path with a shield slung over his shoulders. I saw him just before Martala shot him through the thigh. He fell to the rocks with a bellow of pain and began to writhe around. We waited for her next arrow, but it did not come.

"Kill him," Altrus hissed up at the pinnacle of rock. We could not see her from where we stood at its base.

"No," I said quickly. "Let him crawl back to his master. Let them take care of him. It will give them occupation."

"Such was my intent," she said softly.

Eventually the man ceased to yell and curse, and began to crawl back down the path on his side, whimpering like a child, his sword and shield discarded, the fletched end of the arrow still projecting from his bloody leg.

"The next time they will come in force," Altrus predicted.

We waited for the rush, but for a long time it did not come. Twilight gave way to night. Fortunately for us, the crescent of the waxing moon was overhead when the sun sank, and offered us enough illumination to see the path. I knew it would not remain so forever. In a few hours the moon would slip below the western rim of the canyon, and then Fayez and his mercenaries would be able to steal upon us in the near-total darkness.

"This is suicide," Altrus whispered from the other side of the canyon entrance. In the moonlight he was no more than a gray outline of a man.

"What do you propose?"

"We rush them without warning. Take them by surprise. With luck we can kill three or four of them, maybe more, and get back up the path before they collect their wits."

"That is a rash plan."

"The girl can give us cover with her bow," he argued.

"Oftentimes victory is achieved merely by waiting for your opponent to commit an error."

"What fool philosopher are you quoting now?"

"Those are my own words."

He grunted in derision. He was impatient to be doing something. I understood his restlessness but did not intend to be the first to make a fatal mistake.

It became evident that Fayez was waiting for full darkness

before attempting to overwhelm us with force. The crescent moon sank ever lower toward the western canyon rim.

"I'm going down the path," Altrus said through the darkness. "Come with me or stay here, as you wish."

Before I could speak to dissuade him, a horrible shriek rang out from below. It took me several moments to realize it had been made by a camel. Men began to shout to each other. More camels sounded bellows of alarm, and behind us our own mounts stirred and shuffled against their tethers.

"Can you see anything, Martala?"

"Nothing, Alhazred. Whatever is happening is around a bend in the path, behind some rocks."

The frenzy of the screams, both from men and beasts, increased, and then began to diminish as one by one, the voices were silenced in mid-shriek.

"Someone comes," the girl said.

I heard the pound of running feet against the rocks of the path, and the *twank* of the girl's bowstring. Renewing my grip on the leather-wrapped hilt of my sword, I readied myself for battle.

Three shadowy figures burst through the gap into the canyon. There was enough light that I recognized Fayez and his supposed children. Altrus immediately engaged Fayez, who defended himself with great skill but no enthusiasm. His head kept turning away from his foe to the pathway. I raised my own sword to fight Kazim, then realized that the young man did not even have a sword. He stood shivering and staring back the way he had come. The girl, Najila, held a curved dagger but made no attempt to use it. She was as spellbound as her brother.

"You fools, let us pass," Fayez cried. "It's coming for us. It will kill all of us."

"A poor ruse to distract me," Altrus said as he closed for the kill.

"Wait," I said. "Martala, don't shoot. Come down here at once. Altrus, stay your sword."

... countless sharp white teeth were revealed.

Altrus hesitated. He very much wanted to kill Fayez, but knew I would not speak for nothing.

"We will not fight you," Fayez cried, casting his sword away. He gestured to his daughter, who dropped her dagger. "Quickly, we must escape. We may only have a few moments. Where is the other way out of this place?"

"There is no other way out," Martala said. She approached with caution, her arrow notched to her bow, but not drawn.

Fayez seemed to sag in upon himself. He stared at me with wild eyes. "Then we are all dead."

Another scream rang out from somewhere along the path. To my ears, it sounded nearer than the others.

"That thing is coming for us," Kazim said. His voice quavered with terror. "We need to hide ourselves."

"Look around you, fool," Altrus said with contempt. "There is nowhere to hide."

"We could climb the rock where I was sitting," Martala suggested.

"That would do us no good," Fayez told her. "The thing can fly."

A man ran around the bend in the path. His leather tunic was shredded, and his bloody arms and shoulders appeared streaked with black in the moonlight. He turned to look behind him and stumbled onto his face. Too weak or terrified to get up, he began to crawl frantically along the path on his belly.

Behind him a kind of shadow floated forward on slowly beating wings that were wider than those of any bird. Its eyes were red sparks. They must have been illuminated by some hellish fire within it, for no reflection of the moonlight would have given such a flame to them. It grinned or snarled silently, and as its lips rolled back from its long snout, countless sharp white teeth were revealed. These appeared solid enough, but its wings and body had a strange vagueness of form, as though composed of smoke.

"Now you see," Fayez said, pointing at the creature. "Now you see."

115

The thing dropped upon the shoulders of the crawling man and sank its talons into the flesh of his back. His scream was cut off by a gurgle in his throat when he died.

"We can fight it," Altrus said.

Fayez laughed hysterically.

"Fool, don't you think we tried? No sword will cut it, no arrow will harm it. They pass through as if it were a mere shadow. But its teeth and talons are real enough to kill."

"Try an arrow on it," I said to Martala.

She needed no urging, but drew and released in one smooth motion. The arrow passed through the creature in the region of what should have been its breast. It clicked against the rock behind and fell from sight. For the first time, the thing turned its bat-like head and looked at us.

I heard Najila softly praying to herself. Kazim stood sobbing like a child. Their father stared at me with wide eyes, shaking his head.

"Follow me," I said with sudden inspiration. "Stay close behind."

They needed no urging. The tone of my voice gave them back their wits. I ran toward the center of the canyon, up the slight rise in the domed floor toward the altar.

"Where are we going?" Altrus demanded.

"That thing is what the Thamud carved on the wall. It is the guardian of the stone. I think it may be what we saw behind us in the desert when we approached Jubbah."

"You did not answer my question."

"Everyone, get into the stone circle that surrounds the altar. Quickly, we have only moments."

They were disinclined to dispute the order, but jostled each other to reach the altar.

"Will the circle protect us?" Martala asked.

"I don't know. It shielded the Thamud, but that was centuries ago."

All this while the flying thing floated on the night air, watching us as a cat watches a mouse that struggles within the compass of its claws. Eddies of black smoke curled off the tips of its leathern wings as it flapped them silently.

Bending down to touch a stone of the ring, I began to walk around the altar, touching each stone as I passed it and mentally willing a fiery radiance into it. To my inner sight the stone seemed to glow red. This change was not visible to the others, but I hoped it would be perceptible to the guardian, which was a thing not of flesh but of concentrated spiritual essence.

When it perceived what I was doing, the creature swiftly darted around the ring to the stones I had yet to touch, but I hastened my pace and managed to touch all of them before it reached them. I stood with my eyes closed so that I would not be distracted, and I visualized all the stones burning with spiritual fire and linked to each other like the pearls in a necklace.

"Alhazred?"

Dimly I heard Altrus. There was concern in his voice. He touched my shoulder, and it almost broke my concentration, but somehow I managed to hold my mental focus.

"Don't touch him again," Martala whispered from my other side. "He needs to concentrate."

None of the others spoke again.

Chapter 17

nly when I felt the sun on my cheeks did I dare to open my eyes. I swayed with fatigue as I looked around.

The flying demon was nowhere inside the canyon. The others had found seats on the altar or on the ground. I saw that Altrus, with his typical foresight, had used strips of cloth to bind the wrists of Fayez and his children behind their backs, and to hobble their ankles.

Both Kazim and Najila appeared to be asleep, along with Martala, but Fayez was watching me.

"You saved all our lives."

"This ring of stones protected the priests of the Thamud when they offered sacrifices to the guardian of the red stone," I told him. "It seemed worth the gamble that they would also protect us."

"I am in your debt, not only for my own life, but for the lives of my children."

"I don't want your gratitude, I want your promise."

"Ask and it shall be given to you."

"Give me your pledge that neither you nor your children shall seek to attack us, or flee from us."

He hesitated for a moment, and I saw swift calculation in his eyes, but he smiled and nodded.

"You have my word."

Altrus sat watching this exchange with a cynical expression.

"Cut them loose," I told him.

He shrugged and used his dagger to cut the bonds from our three captives.

"Why don't we just kill them?" he murmured to me as he passed near.

"I heard that," Fayez said.

"They are in the employ of a powerful man, and a member of the royal family. I do not wish to invoke his displeasure if I can avoid it."

"You are trying to steal what he covets out from under him. I think it is safe to assume he will be displeased with you."

"Your mercenary has a point," Fayez said.

In truth, I did not know why I hesitated to kill the three of them while they were still bound like goats. Some instinct counseled against it, and I have learned to trust my instincts. Perhaps it was only a disinclination to take an irrevocable step where no such step was yet needed. I would have had no reluctance to kill Fayez and his broodlings in battle, but murder in cold blood is something I do only when necessary.

The murmur of our voices woke Martala. She yawned, squinted around, and took up her bow.

"Has the demon gone?"

"It cannot harm us by daylight, or it would already have slain us on our approach to Ghouwtah. At night we will be vulnerable, and must take precautions," I told her.

"I have seen it on the heights of Jabal Umm Sanman at twilight," Fayez said. "It always kept its distance, so I never got a clear look at it."

"It probably only attacks when one of the Thamud holy places is violated. The rock carvings show that this is where the stone was once adored."

"You are assuming there is only one guardian," Martala said. "It may be that there are two of them, or even more. How do we know that there is not such a creature set over every Thamud holy place?"

I made no answer to her, since I had none. In a practical

sense it hardly mattered. If Fayez had seen it on the other mountain, then either there were two of the things, or this one had the ability to travel over great distances. Either way, we faced the same threat.

"Will it follow us when we leave?" Altrus asked.

"I don't know. Its reasoning will not be the same as ours."

"It killed all of my men," Fayez said. Fear was beginning to give way to anger in his voice. "Why did it attack us and not you?"

"That is simple enough," Altrus told him. "If it had attacked us first, you would have fled away from the mountain. It knew we had no other way of escape but down the path, where it would be waiting for us. It wanted to kill us all."

We spent part of the morning searching the canyon to be certain the stone was not hidden somewhere within it, but we found nothing. I gave Fayez back his sword, and the three of them retrieved their other weapons from where they had dropped them in their terror.

They proved to be amiable companions. If they harboured resentment against us it was well concealed. Martala and Najila were soon chattering about fashions, and Kazim made a sincere effort to engage Altrus in a discussion of military tactics. Their father and I talked in a casual way about the Persian poets of the past two centuries. He was well-read and a charming conversationalist. There was nothing to show that the three had not resigned themselves completely to their captivity. It is needless to add that I trusted them no further than the reach of my dagger.

Two of the camels that had carried Fayez and his mercenaries to Ghouwtah were still alive, though one of them had a nasty slash on the side of its neck that had clotted up during the night. Fayez took the injured animal, and Kazim sat with Najila behind him on the other. The way they touched and pressed against each other so intimately seemed unnatural for brother and sister, but who am I to censor the habits of others?

We left the mountain with no regret and rode west,

back toward Jubbah. Every so often I would stop and turn in my saddle to scan the horizon behind us, searching for movement through the shimmering mirages that lay over the plain like silver lakes. I saw several dust devils, but none of them remained fixed in its place or behaved in an unnatural way.

Some little distance from Jubbah's gates we stopped. Fayez stayed his camel beside mine.

"Will you enter with me and take wine at my house?" Fayez asked me.

"We would be arrested."

He waved his hand in a negligent manner. "I will talk with Hafiz. He will muzzle his dog, Trievos. You will be safe enough, you have my assurance."

"Many thanks for your generosity, but we must go to the mountain."

He laid his hand on my arm.

"Alhazred, let us speak honestly. I know you go to seek the red stone. Let us go with you. Who knows what dangers you may confront. The flying creature who killed my men may be the least of your foes."

"You would fight to defend one you once tried to have killed with a poisoned dagger?"

"Things have changed. You saved my life and the lives of my children. You spared us when you could have put us to the sword. Yes, I will fight to defend you and your companions. I swear to it."

I would rather have put a viper in my own sleeping blanket than trust this eloquent and sophisticated man at my back, but there were other considerations. He was correct that we had no notion of what forces might be arrayed against us under the mountain. Extra swords might make the difference between securing the stone or violent death. And if I allowed him to ride back into Jubbah, how could I know that he would not inflame the mayor against me? I had no wish to see Trievos riding after me with an angry group of his fellow townsmen.

"Very well, you may come with us to the mountain, if you and you children swear to be led by me and to abide by my decisions."

All three solemnly swore an oath. I looked into their faces for signs of deceit but they appeared sincere. I noticed Altrus frowning at me from behind their camels. When he saw my eye upon him he merely shook his head with a grim expression.

We turned from the open gates of the town and rode around its wall toward the looming slope of Jabal Umm Sanman. It was late afternoon, our camels were exhausted, and we all wanted to rest, but I was flaming inside with a passion to curl my fingers around the neck of the witch, Salamagoogah. The red stone was somewhere beneath her lair. She had known this all along, but had sent me to Ghouwtah in the assurance that the demon would end my life. For that I would strangle her with my own hands.

Chapter 18

With our camels hobbled and staked in a gully at the base of the mountain, we climbed the slope toward the cave of the witch. Fayez had never been inside the cave or even suspected its existence, but he knew the way to the summit with assurance, having spent the past six months combing the mountain for Thamud rock carvings. We reached the cleft shortly after the setting of the sun, while the sky was still lit with pale light. It was the hour when the witch walked abroad on the mountain, but we had no assurance she was not still within her den.

I approached cautiously with my dagger drawn. There was no space in the narrow entrance passage to swing a sword. The others came behind me, Martala immediately behind and Altrus at the rear where he could watch everyone. Down and down we crept into the bowels of the mountain. Every dozen steps I stopped and listened with stilled breath, but there was no sound.

As before, an oil lamp burned in the cavern Salamagoogah made her home, but the witch was absent.

"She must have left the cave at twilight, before we reached it," I murmured. The weight of the mountain above me made me hush my voice. It pressed on my chest like the hand of an invisible giant. Even so, my words echoed from the rock walls and vaulted ceiling of the chamber.

"We can lie in wait and kill her when she returns," Najila said.

"That we cannot do," her father said in admonishment. "It may be that she is the only person in the world who knows the exact location of the red stone. She must be tortured until we extract whatever information about its resting place she possesses. Then we will kill her."

"Of course, Father, how stupid of me."

My fingers tightened around the hilt of my dagger as I thought about sliding its blade into the witch, but I knew he spoke wisdom. As much as I longed to kill her, we must keep her alive until she told us how to find the stone. If she would not give up the information freely, she must be encouraged by whatever means were needed.

All this while, Altrus had ranged from one side of the cavern to another with the oil lamp in his hand, sniffing the air like a hound on the scent. He stopped abruptly and held the lamp close to the keyhole in the door of the wooden cabinet. The flame fluttered. He did not need to call to us. We all stood watching him, the words on our lips forgotten in our sudden excitement.

I tried to tip the cabinet over but it was fastened securely to the rock wall behind it. With the blades of our daggers we were able to pry the door open. The brass lock broke with a loud crack and the door swung wide to reveal a tunnel opening into the rock behind. It was a low hole no more than half the height of a man.

"I wonder where this leads?" Altrus said.

"Have a care; she may be down there."

"Only one way to find out." He grinned at me and dropped to his knees, then crawled awkwardly into the hole with the lamp held in one hand.

Martala did not hesitate, but immediately followed him, her little dagger clamped between her teeth and her bow and quiver clutched to her breast.

I gestured for Fayez to follow her. After a moment's hesitation, he looked at his son and jerked his head. Kazim crawled in after the girl, and his sister followed at his heels.

"We may be crawling to our deaths," Fayez said.

"Every man born of woman begins to crawl to his death the day he drops from his mother's womb."

"You are a philosopher, Alhazred, but philosophy is cold comfort when death presses near."

"The others will be waiting for us."

With a deep exhalation, he shook his head and crawled into the now darkened passage. I did not wait but hastened to follow after him, conscious of a prickling sensation between my shoulder blades.

There was a glimmer in front of me on the sides of the rocks, made by the fluttering flame of the lamp in Altrus's hand. The passage descended like a writhing serpent but the floor was flat, which indicated to me that it had been at least partially cut by men. No natural cave has a flat floor. Nor were there any stone spurs jutting down from the roof on which to bash out my brains. The passage had been smoothed with hammers and chisels by men who knew how to shape stone.

At length it became possible to stand erect, although the tunnel continued to descend at a steep incline. Each of us laid a hand on the shoulder of the person in front, and we followed Altrus in silence, like dead souls escorted on their way to the Greek Underworld.

I do not know what I expected to find at the end of the tunnel. Perhaps a cavern filled with old bones. Whatever my anticipation, it was not the echoing vastness into which we walked behind the lamp. Its dancing flame cast dim shadows over two rows of fluted pillars of enormous girth and height. Even when Altrus raised the lamp high in his hand, the tops of these pillars could not be glimpsed, but faded into shadow and darkness.

"I have not seen the like since leaving Egypt," Martala said in a voice of wonder.

Indeed, the pillars reminded me of the great pillars at Karnack in the land of the Nile. They were not quite so massive, but the difference was trifling.

"To think this lay below the mountain all the time I searched above it," Fayez said in disgust.

"None knew of it save the witch," Altrus said.

He carried the lamp between two of the pillars to the wall of the great hall, and after a moment a second flame sprang to life.

"There are lamps set in the walls, and they are filled with oil."

"Salamagoogah must have filled them," I murmured, "But for what purpose?"

One after the other, Altrus lit all the lamps along both side walls of the hall. Their combined radiance was not enough to show the ceiling, which was lost in the gloom above, but it did reveal an open passage at the far end carved in the shape of a temple entrance. I noted that the pillars had not been lifted into place in blocks, but were chiseled from the seamless stone of the mountain. The great hall had been hollowed out, probably from some existing cavern. It must have been the work of generations.

"This is where the Thamud dwelt," I said with sudden insight. "We looked for entrances to their houses on the sides of the mountain, but they made their home in its depths."

"Let's go on," Fayez said eagerly. "The red stone may be just ahead of us."

By the uncertain glow of the wall lamps I saw something move in the depths of shadow at the far end of the passage. Before I could cry out a warning, the opening erupted with hundreds of creatures, like a mouth that vomits filth. They were of small stature, naked, and a sickly gray-white in color. All of them, both male and female, were hairless. They had no eyes, but only tightly closed slits where their eyes should have been. As if in compensation, their ears and mouths were larger than normal, and their flattened noses were grotesquely wide. The most inhuman aspect of these creatures was their silence. They did not cry out as they threw themselves upon us but attacked mutely.

We were caught by surprise. Even so, we managed to slay more than a score of them before they overwhelmed us with sheer force of numbers and bore us down to the floor of the hall. Our weapons were snatched from our hands. For a time I could see nothing except the writhing bodies that pressed me against the stone. Cold, damp hands covered my face, blocked my vision, and stifled my nose and mouth, so that I feared I would be suffocated under them.

Dimly I was aware of the lamps in the hall being snuffed out one by one, as if by someone who walked up one side and down the other. As each lamp failed, the hall grew blacker.

"Alhazred!" I recognized Martala's voice.

"Here," I managed to shout before my mouth was covered. The naked, dank bodies pressed against me made me shudder in an involuntary spasm of revulsion. I am not a man easily revulsed. The girl's terror must have been overwhelming.

The pale white things dragged me across the floor on my back and stood me up against one of the pillars. My arms were forced behind me and my wrists bound with some kind of sinew or gut. So great was the thickness of the pillar that my hands did not meet on the other side. I stood listening to the sound of naked skin sliding along skin and stone. It was a serpent-like sound, not made by a single being, but by hundreds of dwarfish men and women who writhed and wriggled against each other like a cluster of maggots feeding on rotten meat. To my surprise, the things gave off very little odor.

They withdrew from the hall, leaving it dark and silent apart from the small noises of my companions.

"Has anyone been injured?" I asked.

All of them denied serious injury. From the location of their voices, I realized that they were tied to pillars, as I had been, three on each side of the central aisle.

"They came out of nowhere," Fayez said through the darkness. "Why haven't they killed us?"

"Maybe they prefer fresh meat," Altrus said, and I heard a trace of humor in his voice.

"That's a horrible thing to say," Najila told him.

"They're not ghouls," I said. "They may not eat human flesh."

"What are they?" Martala asked.

"The Thamud. We were mistaken to believe they had all vanished. They were here all the while, living and breeding beneath the mountain. The witch told me, but I paid little heed to her words."

"There were hundreds of the monsters," Fayez said in disgust. "What do they use for food?"

"Did you see their eyes?" his son, Kazim, asked in a voice that trembled with horror. "They are all blind."

"Living for generations in total darkness, they would have no need for eyes," I said in what I hoped was a soothing tone. To judge by his voice, the young man stood swaying on the brink of howling madness.

"We're not alone," Altrus said.

"What do you mean?" Najila demanded.

"Someone is listening to us."

We all fell silent and strained our hearing. A chuckle of delight came through the darkness from one end of the hall. I recognized the voice of the witch.

"Salamagoogah, release us," I said.

For a time there was no answer. Then a woman said softly, as though talking to herself, "So many playthings. So many playthings."

Chapter 19

The voice of the witch chilled my blood. We were her possessions, and she intended to amuse herself with us. In what ways, I did not care to imagine. Yet we were not molested for several hours, but left to dangle in the darkness at the sides of the pillars.

"This did not work out quite as I had hoped," I said to break the quiet.

Fayez laughed harshly, and I heard somebody spit—probably Kazim.

"There was no way to know anything lived down here other than the witch," Altrus said.

"Salamagoogah told me the Thamud were still down here. I should have listened."

Another brooding silence descended upon us. Martala broke it.

"Alhazred, do you believe the red stone resides here?"

"I have no doubt that it does. Why else would the Thamud have continued to dwell in this cave if it were not to guard the stone and worship it?"

"The witch is in league with them."

"So it appears. She must have formed some pact with the creatures long ago."

"Do you think she means to kill us?"

"She cannot let us leave the mountain. We know her secret."

The next silence endured a long time. I slept, how many

hours I have no way to judge, and opened my eyes to the same drear blackness. My hands were completely numb, which was a relief after the pain, but I knew I would lose both of them if the sinew that bound my wrists were not soon cut away. The same was probably true for the others, who to their credit voiced no complaint. I heard soft snores and grunts from them as they slept on their feet, and did not speak for fear of awakening them from the blessings of sleep.

Someone comes, Sashi said in my mind.

I heard it then, the soft brush of bare feet over smooth stone. The steps ceased near me, and I felt a presence and scented a subtle odor I had smelled before.

"Have you come to gloat, Salamagoogah?"

"No," she said out of the darkness. "Not to gloat."

She spoke several soft, sibilant words in a language unknown to me, and two of the naked creatures grasped my arms from either side of the pillar. I felt my bonds cut away, and my arms were released. I stood swaying with fatigue and peeled the remnants of the cords from the indentations they had made in my wrists. My fingers were without feeling. I fumbled for a long time to accomplish this simple task, and by the time I finished it, the pricking needles had begun to torment my fingertips. The blood was returning to my hands. I welcomed the agony.

"Take my hand. I will lead you."

Extending my prickling, swollen fingers, I felt her grasp them. Her grip was surprisingly strong for the hand of a woman. She drew me after her down the hall toward the unseen entrance that was carved like a temple doorway. If any of the others woke and heard our words, they made no sound to show it.

"Where are you taking me?"

"To a place were we can talk together in comfort."

This was unexpected. I could not conceive what the witch would need to talk to me about. She had all of us in her power. I had expected her to amuse herself by torturing and killing us.

For a brief moment I considered putting my hands around her slender neck and choking the life out of her. It was just possible I could accomplish it before her blind guardians realized what I was doing. What stopped me was curiosity. I wanted to know what she would say to me.

I had a sense of being led across a vast yet empty cavern. The only sounds were our shuffling footfalls. The very air itself seemed to listen to our passage, and I felt disapproval emanate from the stone walls. If ever a place could be said to possess its own malign awareness, it was this place.

Through the dark I saw a thin rectangle of light that indicated a door. She opened this and drew me into a well-furnished chamber with rugs on the stone floor, tapestries hanging from the walls, and a low couch covered in soft cushions. On the table beside this couch were silver bowls containing figs, dates, oranges, grapes, and other delicacies. Red wine sparkled in a crystal decanter, lit by the light of a large oil lamp with five wicks. The lamp, which was of gold, had the look of some temple artifact. I noticed that the tapestries and rugs were of extreme age.

She murmured in the same unknown tongue I had heard her use earlier, and the crouching white creatures felt their way out the door and closed it behind them, leaving me alone with the witch.

"You are very trusting," I said.

"Several hundred of the Thamud are within the sound of my voice," she said with a smile. "In any case, you are no threat to me."

As much as I longed to teach her the error of her words, I merely curled my fingers into fists and smiled in return.

"Sit, Alhazred. I have a proposition to make to you."

Wondering where this could possibly lead, I took a seat on one end of the couch, and she stretched herself out on the other end, extending her long, sleek legs with her bare arm over the back of the couch.

"By now you have deduced that the red stone exists, and that I possess it," she said.

"Yes."

"You must realize that I could not permit you to take it away. For one thing, it is the source of my longevity. Were it removed far from my presence for more than a few days, I would die. And then there is the threat that it poses to the world."

"What threat do you speak about?"

"Should the red stone and the black stone be reunited without the mediating influence of the white stone, this entire terrestrial globe would be rent by cataclysmic disasters the magnitude of which no man could imagine. So say the legends."

"White stone?"

She laughed.

"Yes: there are three stones, not two, as you very well know. They all function as independent entities. The black stone, the right hand of God, as it is called, gives spiritual wisdom and prosperity. The red stone, or left hand of God, is the stone of severe judgment and punishment. It gives invulnerability and dominion over all the lands and peoples of this world."

"Does the red stone make you invulnerable?"

"No. To me it gives the gift of long life, so long as I serve it as guardian. To the man who holds it in his hand, it gives invulnerability from fire and sword and any earthly harm, but only so long as he possesses it."

"What is the function of the white stone?"

"It is said that it balances the forces of the other two, and for this reason it is known as the heart of God. Alone, it has the power to heal the sickness of those who touch it, but when united with the other two stones, it brings about an age of peace and love across the entire world that lasts ten thousand years, or so the legend promises."

"Where is this white stone?"

She laughed, a musical sound that thrilled me in spite of my wariness of her.

"No one knows. There are rumors, but I believe it has been lost. And therein lies the danger, for the legends say that if the black stone is united with the red stone, without the moderating influence of the white stone, all of creation will fall to ruin and ashes."

I considered her words. It was only a legend, and most legends were false, but if there were any truth in it, for me to bear the red stone back to Damascus and give it to the Caliph might not be the wisest course. It was not unlikely that he would take it to Mecca to be reunited with the black stone of the Ka'bah.

She reached out her hand to touch my cheek, and began to caress the line of my jaw.

"Such a pity that your beauty was spoiled."

I realized that I had not renewed the glamour that masked my true face. She stopped me as I began to make the ritual gesture.

"No, leave it as it is. We all have our scars, whether they be exposed to the eyes of others or concealed in darkness."

Her liquid green eyes were sensual, her touch cool and delightful. Only a block of wood could fail to grasp her intention. I wondered how she would react when she knew that I was a eunuch. To delay that moment, I continued to talk.

"What is your connection with the stone? Why do you dwell here in darkness? Is it only to extend your years of life?"

"I am bound to the stone by ancient oaths," she said. "Oaths so terrible that it would terrify you just to hear their terms."

"Then why don't you use the stone to conquer a kingdom? You could rule from a high throne instead of hiding beneath this mountain."

She smiled and shook her head. "Alas, I cannot touch the stone. I am female, and no female creature may touch the red stone and live. In order to unleash its power of conquest, it is necessary to carry it close to the skin, and were I to even brush against it, I would surely perish."

A glimmer of her purpose began to enter my mind. She reached up and toyed with the lobe of my ear.

"The men of the Thamud can touch the stone, but they have degenerated too greatly from their former Persian nobility to be able to use its power, even with the help of my wisdom."

"You need a man who can wield the stone on your behalf," I said.

"Precisely. You cannot imagine how long I have waited to find the right man. Sending you to Ghouwtah was merely a test of your mettle. You passed the test by surviving and returning here. Now I know that you are fit to rule beside me. Together we can use the red stone to conquer the world. The conquests of Mohammed, even those of Alexander, will be as nothing to our dominion."

"Do you mean to overthrow the Caliphate?"

"All caliphs, all kings, all despots, will be cast down to grovel at our feet for scraps from our table. You cannot conceive the limitless power of the stone, but I will teach you how to wield it as a weapon against which no prince or god can prevail."

"What will happen to my companions?"

She shrugged indifferently.

"If you agree to serve me, I will allow them to keep their lives. Their fate is of no consequence to me. If you refuse, they will supply me with sport and meat for many days."

"Do the Thamud also eat the flesh of men?"

"The Thamud subsist on a fungus that grows in the deep caverns. It has almost no taste. I prefer bloody flesh."

"As do I."

"I saw you talking with the ghouls in the burial ground, and wondered about your purpose."

"They led me to your cave. Without them I would never have found you."

"How interesting. Remind me to take the time some night to enter their warren and kill them all."

Whether this was an idle boast, I did not ask. I talked on of inconsequential matters to delay my decision until I considered her offer. It might have tempted me more if I relished dominion over other men, but the truth was that the lives of others bored me. I had no wish to tell them what to do or what not to do. I only wanted to be left alone and free to live my life as I chose to live it, and that blessing I already possessed in my house at Damascus.

"We shall conquer together, slay together, and lie together," she said, her green eyes shining as she gazed past me into the limitless land of the future. "From my eternally fertile womb shall arise a dynasty of kings the like of which this world has never known."

"An intriguing prospect," I said, conscious of the emptiness between my thighs.

"We should couple together now, to consecrate our future union."

I stood up quickly.

"First, show me this red stone so that I know you have not spoken fables into my ear."

She uncoiled her legs and slid easily to her feet like a rearing serpent.

"I will take you to it at once, so that you may touch it and feel its power coursing through your body."

Excellent, I thought. *And when I hold it in my hand, I will use it to dash in your skull.*

I smiled, and she returned my smile like a lover.

Chapter 20

She led me back into the echoing, open space that watched and listened. I was not conscious of anyone else present, but a few murmured words from her lips in the language of the white creatures was enough to set them lighting lamps around the perimeter of the cavern.

As the flames of the lamps kindled, I saw that it was not a natural cavern, but that it had been fashioned by men. It was perfectly round, with a domed ceiling so high that its apex was shrouded in shadow. Openings all around it led off into unlit passageways. One of these must extend to the hall of pillars where my companions were bound, but I could not determine which, for they were all identical.

In the center of the floor arose a kind of pyramid cut from the living stone of the mountain. All around on its four sides were flights of steps leading up to its flat top. This was so high above my head that I could not see what rested there.

Salamagoogah led me by the hand up the steps. The platform at the top was some ten paces across. Upon an oblong recumbent block of stone rested what appeared to be an Egyptian mummy. At least to my eyes, the wrapping of narrow linen strips seemed to have been applied in the Egyptian manner. I had seen how it was done while in Egypt. The hands of the figure were gathered together on its breast, and I was reminded of the carving in the blind canyon on Ghouwtah that depicted a similar mummy with the red stone shining between its hands.

Releasing the fingers of the witch, I approached this strange tomb, for such it must be. In the dim glow that reached upward from the lamps around the cavern wall, I saw that the shrunken and dried fingers of the corpse were not wrapped. They grasped something that resembled a large egg of a dull red color.

"It does not glow," I murmured. The weight of the shadows in that place made me speak softly.

"It only glows when held by a living man."

"If it grants deathlessness, why is the one who holds it a shriveled corpse?"

She came nearer until she stood beside me. I could not help but be aware of her scent, which was intoxicating.

"This man never held the stone in life. He was its keeper, but he feared to touch it. When the stone was moved, it was supported on a sling made of linen. Only after the keeper died of extreme old age was he afforded the honor of having the stone placed between his hands."

I bent close and sniffed the spices that were bound into the wrappings of the mummy. The cloth was covered in a fine green mold and a layer of dust. It might not reside in Egypt, but this mummy was as old as many that lay entombed on the banks of the Nile.

"How do you know all these things?"

"I was the keeper's concubine."

Turning my head, I studied her finely shaped features and the unmarked ivory of her skin.

"The years rest lightly upon you."

"Say not years, but centuries."

"Why do you play the witch of the mountain?"

"It is necessary to keep watch on the comings and goings of the men of Jubbah, and those few from the caravans who dare to climb its slope. The Thamud have no eyes, so the task falls to me. Besides, I enjoy walking beneath the moon and stars."

"You are not what you seem to be," I said, stepping away from her.

"None of us are what we seem. We all wear masks of different kinds that suit our needs. Of all men you should know that."

"What is it you want from me?"

"Only that you take up the stone, hold it in your hands, and feel its power."

"You cannot take it up?'

"I've already told you, it would blast me to cinders."

"But it will not harm me?"

"On the contrary, Alhazred, it will transform you into a god."

My intention was to seize the stone, kill the witch, and free my companions from their pillars. It was not a complex plan, yet something made me hesitate. I rubbed my palms together and discovered that they were sweating.

"Don't be afraid. The stone has waited for you for centuries. Pick it up."

My love, do not touch it, Sashi whispered in my mind.

The times I have disregarded Sashi's warnings are few in number, and always I have regretted it. Yet I could not have stopped my hand from straying toward the stone on the breast of the corpse even if I had wished. Some attraction greater than my will set my fingers on its smooth surface.

For a moment, nothing happened. Then a tide of warmth washed up my arm through my blood and flesh and into my chest. From there it spread to all my extremities. I felt stronger. Drawing a deep breath, I was aware of my body taking the good from the air and carrying it to my heart, which beat with a more powerful rhythm, slow and deep. My mind became clear. All the clutter of half-forgotten worries and cares was swept away as if by a great wind that blows dust out the open windows and doors of a house, and suddenly I found that I could see beyond the mass of the mountain that surrounded me.

My gaze flashed across the desert to Damascus and into the palace of the Caliph, who I saw sitting in his study, reading a scroll. He was such a simple man. He had the mind

... the stone had begun to glow a dull red ...

of a small boy that sees injustice and wants only to right it. Little wonder his reign was so perilous. He would be an easy conquest.

Turning my thoughts, I sent my gaze south to Mecca, where men tended the Ka'bah, and saw its black stone set in its silver frame. Soon the red and black would be united. My armies would sweep across Arabia like a desert wind and no prince would stand before me.

From Mecca, I cast my gaze to the north and the west, even to far off Constantinople, where I looked through the doors of the mother church and saw the pontiff upon his papal throne. Once Arabia was under my banner, it would be time to turn my armies toward Christendom.

All this I saw in the space of an instant. Returning to the tomb, I realized that the stone had begun to glow a dull red against my fingertips, yet it did not burn me. In the back of my head I heard and felt a kind of throbbing pulse. With careless disregard, I ripped away the desiccated fingers of the corpse and took up the stone in my left hand. Raising it high, I shouted from the sheer exhilaration of its power.

The witch recoiled from me in wonder, and mingled with her admiration I could feel her fear. She had known the power of the stone, but knowing a thing and experiencing it are not the same. I repented of my intention to kill her. She could serve me as a useful instrument. A master does not wantonly kill his slaves.

The red light of the stone increased until it filled the enormous domed cavern. It was too intense to look upon. Before I even knew what I intended, I called out a command in the lost language of the Thamud, which by some magic of the stone I understood. My voice thundered from the dome above my head like the voice of a god.

From all the openings in the sides of the cavern poured forth the naked white creatures. They milled around the steps of the tomb in confusion and growing excitement. Although blind, in some manner they could feel the power of the stone, awakened for the first time in centuries. I spoke to them in their own tongue, promising them glory and plunder, as had been their forefathers' in the days of old. The creatures shook their fists in the air and opened their mouths to scream their approval.

These creatures would be my first soldiers. I would go forth from the mountain and persuade the ghouls to also fight beneath my banner. The oasis would serve as a useful base from which to extend my power across Arabia. When we had conquered Jubbah, I would have men and camels and could send out emissaries calling the princes of the land to serve me.

All this I saw with absolute clarity in the space of a moment. Inside me there was no room for doubt or questions. The fire of the stone filled my body with a burning need to conquer and rule. So must Alexander have felt when he gazed upon the walls of Babylon.

I perceived that the witch was staring at my face in wonder. I turned my gaze to her, and she quailed beneath its majesty.

"Why do you stare?"

"The stone has made you whole. It has restored you."

Touching my nose, I laughed with delight. I reached between my legs and felt what stood forth there erect, hot and hard, throbbing with the passion of life itself. My ears, too, had returned, and my cheeks were healed. All of the parts of my body that old King Huban of Sana'a in Yemen had cut off as punishment for violating the virtue of his daughter, Narisa, were back again. I looked at the witch and felt the sudden urge to throw her down upon the steps and rape her, but I controlled my lust. There would be time enough for that after I had formed the seeds of my army.

"Alhazred, what are you doing?"

I recognized the voice of Altrus above the frenzied screams of the naked white hoard that milled around the steps of the tomb. Somehow the others had freed themselves from their pillars and found their weapons where they had been put.

The Thamud heard his voice and immediately turned to attack.

"Hold," I called out in their language. "Bring the barbarians to me."

The witch did not dare to contradict me. A sense of order fell over the blind creatures. They were at a disadvantage in the light, but they massed their numbers on either side of the five and cut off their retreat back out the passage from which they had issued.

"If you fight them, they will fall upon you in their numbers and tear you to pieces," I told Altrus.

They allowed the Thamud to push them forward to the steps of the tomb. I stood looking down upon them with amusement.

"How did you escape the pillars?"

"I cut them free," Martala said. She held up her little dagger.

My laughter rang upon the air. Of course, I should have guessed. The girl's little dagger, which no one ever seemed able to find when they searched her. The Thamud had not taken it from her.

"But how did you get it to your bonds?"

Martala kicked off one of her boots, took the hilt of the dagger between her toes, and bent her leg back behind her so that the blade of the dagger was near her buttocks. I nodded with appreciation. She looked at me strangely as she pulled her boot back on.

"Alhazred," Altrus said hesitantly. "What is wrong with your eyes?"

I raised my right hand to my face. "What about my eyes?"

"They are ... glowing."

Holding my fingers close, I saw that indeed there was a red glow upon them.

"It is the red stone," I told him. "It has renewed me and made me a god."

They looked at each other uneasily.

Fayez stepped forward to attract my notice. "I ask only one thing, O Lord, that you allow me and my children to serve you."

For a moment I actually considered his request. I needed

men who could swing a sword or shoot a bow, but his deceit knew no bounds.

"Separate yourself and your children from these two others," I said.

He bowed deeply.

"Thank you, my Lord, and rest assured, our service shall always please you."

When they were far enough away from Altrus and Martala, I spoke a few words to the Thamud in their own tongue. They surrounded Fayez and his offspring, finding them by sound, scent and touch, then began to howl as they tore them into bloody pieces of flesh with their long fingernails. In moments the floor at the base of the tomb was a pool of blood. As ordered, they brought me the head of the old man.

I held it up by the hair in my right hand and examined it closely by the radiance of the stone, wondering if the brain inside that skull was still active, and whether the eyes that stared back at me saw my face, or the ears heard my voice.

"You tried to assassinate me in my bed," I told him. "If you thought your life would ever end in any other way than this, you were a fool."

I threw the head back down to the foot of the stair, and the Thamud, aroused by the scent of blood, began to kick it with their feet and smear their bodies with redness, all the while howling like demons.

Chapter 21

"The ghoul clans all across Arabia must be united under my banner. They will become my eyes and ears in the night, and more than this, my assassins."

We had retired to one of Salamagoogah's private rooms to plot strategy. My brain was afire with schemes and ploys. Martala and Altrus were with us. I had called them there against the wishes of the witch because I wanted a sword at my back that I could depend on. They stood uneasily together at the other side of the chamber, watching us warily. The change in my nature frightened them. It was to be expected. They would become accustomed to it soon enough.

"I will go to the warren of the Green Earth Clan and speak with their leader, Bakka. He will listen to my words."

"No," the witch said. "It ill befits the ruler of the world to go in person to beg for terms from those he will command. You must send an emissary."

I laughed lightly. She thought she was subtle, but the radiance of the stone enabled me to read her purposes with ease. She did not want me to go out of her presence for fear that I would escape her control. She did not yet realize that it was I who controlled her.

"Anyone I send is apt to be killed. The ghouls do not like men to intrude into their territory at night."

"Send me," Altrus said. "I am not afraid of any ghoul."

I studied him. A lesser man I would have suspected of seeking only to flee back to Jubbah to warn its residents of the horde that would soon descend upon them, or even more basely, to secure a camel and flee across the desert. But I knew no such craven thoughts existed in the heart of the mercenary, who was as fearless as any man that lived.

"Take this," I told him, and awkwardly untied Gor's skull from my belt with my right hand. The stone still nestled in my left, glowing with soft red light, and its weight seemed as nothing to me. I felt a curious reluctance to set it down. It would be necessary to make some kind of sling to carry it at my waist, as I carried Gor's skull, but for now I found no effort in holding it in my hand.

He took the skull and tied the thong attached to it around his own belt.

"Are you sure this is what you want?" he murmured to me while I was close and the witch was out of hearing.

"You cannot conceive how much I want this. Look, it has made my body whole." I touched my nose. "In the same way it has augmented my mind and made it stronger and wiser. We will ride together across this wide world, and bring it to its knees as Alexander did a thousand years ago. Nothing will stand against us. You will have wealth and lands beyond your greatest desires. A kingdom shall be yours, to rule over at my right hand."

"Do you not feel ill, Alhazred?" Martala whispered as she came near. "You are so changed in your speech."

"It is the power of the stone," I told her. "I would let you touch it, and then you would understand, but no woman may touch the red stone and live."

"What are you saying to each other?" the witch asked sharply.

"They congratulate me," I told her. To Altrus I said, "Take care in the burial ground. Go to the far corner where the oldest graves are and wait. When you sense them near, hold up Gor's skull and tell them you have come as my emissary with a proposal that will please them. Ask to be taken to see Bakka and go with them." I grasped his arm. "But at the slightest hint of betrayal, slay as many ghouls as you can and flee back to the mountain."

"It will be as you wish."

"Tell the Thamud to escort him to the surface unharmed," I told Salamagoogah. She stared at me coldly, but went to do as I commanded. Altrus followed after her.

Martala and I stood alone together in the chamber, which was bare apart from a low couch and a chair. The floor was covered with one of those ancient, moldy rugs the Thamud had brought with them from Persia. I wondered that it had not fallen to dust, but reflected that in this place almost no feet walked upon it.

The girl appeared nervous to approach me.

"There is nothing to fear," I told her in an imitation of my old voice.

"When the stone restored your body, did it restore you ... down there?"

I laughed at her hesitation.

"Yes, even down there."

"Do you mean it's real? It's not just a glamour?"

"Come and touch it if you wish. It's real enough. I look forward to using it again. It has been far too long."

I felt my prick crawl between my thighs as it began to fill with blood. It was eager to stand erect at the slightest excuse. The girl started to extend her hand but then drew it back nervously, staring into my eyes.

"I am happy for you, Alhazred."

"I know you are. You and Altrus are the only ones I can trust here. That is why I want you close to me at all times. Keep your eye on the witch. She needs me to wield the stone, but she thinks that there is no need for you to be alive. She may try to kill you."

"Let her try," the girl said with her usual fire of spirit. This pleased me. Above all I needed to surround myself with warriors.

What of you, Sashi? I asked in my mind. *You have been strangely silent. Can I count on you to fight beside me in this coming war of conquest?*

I am with you unto death, my love, she said, but the face she materialized in the air before me was sad.

Do not be disheartened. We will still make love as we did of old.

My sorrow is for you, Alhazred.

Sad, for me? There is no cause. Rather, be joyous. My life has become filled with purpose.

Are you sure it is your purpose, and not the stone's?

Her question confused me for a moment. I frowned and shook my head to clear it. *Speak not to me again until I rule Jubbah,* I thought. *Your words distract me, and I must plan for war.*

Altrus would not return until tomorrow night. This night was largely spent and ghouls could not travel under the sun. At my suggestion the girl laid herself down on the witch's couch and soon fell asleep.

I was too energized for sleep. I traced the passage up to the outer cavern of the witch without meeting her. There I found a split waterskin and used her knife to cut it into a makeshift sling for the red stone, which I tied to my belt. It hung where Gor's skull had once hung, glowing with dull redness, and emitted a kind of hum that thrilled through the bones of my head when I stroked it. The effect was not so potent as when I held it in my hand.

I went out onto the summit of the mountain and found a place to sit where I could listen to the sounds of the desert and watch the stars. Yet I scarcely heard or saw these things. In my eyes were visions of conquest over great cities and sea battles that involved a thousand warships. In my ears rang steel against steel and the dying screams of men as I contemplated my future course. It stretched before me like a broad, straight road. I knew exactly what steps I needed to take to begin and carry forth the conquest of the world, and the prospect did not daunt me in the least. I yearned to make the stars wheel faster through the heavens so that I might more swiftly set my plans into motion.

"May I sit beside you?"

The witch had approached me from behind without making a sound, but I had smelled her scent and was not startled.

"Do you now ask my permission, when so recently you held me captive?"

She sat on my left side.

"Have a care for the stone, lest you brush against it."

"I am ever aware of the red stone, Alhazred."

Even so, I untied it from my belt and held the sling in my right hand. I felt a reluctance to actually set it down on the rock, and the more I considered doing so, the stronger the reluctance became, so I simply held it.

The witch placed her hand on my chest and pressed me back until I was lying on the domed ledge. She lay beside me and pressed herself close against my left side. I felt her warmth. She began to kiss my neck and cheek, playfully tickling my skin with the tip of her tongue.

My body responded in a natural way. My restored prick filled with blood and lifted its head against the fabric of my thawb.

"What have we here?" she said as she reached up along my thigh.

"A long-lost friend that has returned to me."

"You speak in riddles."

"Do not try to understand me, witch. Your simplistic schemes and plots are as transparent to me as the air we breathe, but you will never know my mind."

Her fingers tightened around my prick, and I felt the sharpness of her fingernails dig into my flesh, but she laughed.

"You are right, my king. I am only a simple female who wants your manhood between her thighs. Come, make a son in my womb."

With a flip of the hem of my thawb, she exposed my body to the waist and then rolled on top of me. Her warm wetness engulfed my prick and swallowed it whole. It was a sensation I had felt before, but one I had not expected to ever feel again.

151

The poets say that the sweetest pleasures in life are those lost, and then rediscovered. I thought about casting her off but could not find a reason. When she stretched herself along my limbs and kissed my mouth, my mind became vacant. She drew the air from between my lips with the passion of her kiss and left me gasping. All the while, she was careful to hold my right forearm in her hand to ensure that the red stone came nowhere near her skin.

The fancy came to me that instead of a beautiful woman, the shadow of a great black wing stretched across my body, beating softly up and down in the night air to the rhythm of my pelvic thrusts.

At last I groaned aloud and released my seed deep into her gaping womb. She continued to lie on top of me until my shrunken manhood slipped from her. Then she rolled to my left side and we lay watching the stars.

"How old did you say you were?" It was a tactless question, but I was angry with myself for so easily succumbing to her charms and in no mood to humor her vanity.

"In truth, I don't remember," she said quietly. There was no resentment in her voice. "I was old when the foundations of Babylon were laid. I have always been with the red stone, following it as it was moved around the world, watching empires rise and fall. Sometimes I sat as a queen upon a golden throne, and held the power of life and death over many men. At other times I huddled in dank caves and waited for the stone to find another man who could wield it. A man like you, Alhazred."

The stars began to pale in the heavens.

"We must return into the mountain," she said.

Pushing herself up to a sitting posture, she looked down into my eyes.

"You have put a man-child in my belly this night. For that I thank you."

"Your thanks are perhaps premature."

She smiled with confidence and shook her head.

"No. Your seed has taken hold within me. I feel it."

Who was I to argue with a witch older than Babylon? In any case, my mind was filled with visions of warfare and conquest. I retied the pouch with the stone to my belt and followed her inside the cleft to sleep through the day.

Chapter 22

e slept together in the outer cavern, where I had shared her stew on our first meeting. When I awoke, I found her feeding her fire with twigs to heat a similar broth. The taste was foul but I ate it anyway. Making my way up the narrow passage and out the cave entrance, I stood on a precipice and relieved my bladder. It gave me pleasure to once again be able to change the direction of the stream of urine. It is the small things in life that we miss the most.

The position of the sun informed me that it was already late afternoon. In two hours or so it would be dark, and Altrus would make his way up the mountain with Bakka and his ghouls, assuming Altrus was still alive. I had confidence in the resourcefulness of the mercenary.

While Salamagoogah slept, I descended into the deep passages and found where my sword and dagger had been put. Carrying them on my belt once again gave me a sense of wholeness. I called the Thamud men to me in the tomb room. Day and night were the same for them. They seemed to have no regular time for sleep. At any rate they came to my call and assembled around the elevated tomb of the mummified keeper of the stone, their heads tilted back, their blind faces turned up to me.

It amazed me to discover that I knew their number merely by looking over them, without the need to count them as individuals. This was yet another gift of the stone. They were somewhat less than seven hundred, including the half-grown younglings.

"Do you have leaders?" I called out in their own language, which my mouth shaped as easily as though I had spoken it all my life.

Eight males of more advanced years shambled forward to the foot of the stairs. I motioned for them to gather in one place.

"Do you possess weapons?"

"We have weapons," the oldest of them said.

"Gather them all and bring them forth."

This took some time. Martala came into the great domed chamber, stepping cautiously around the blind Thamud, who were aware of her presence but ignored her as though she did not exist. She mounted the stairs of the tomb and stood beside me.

"Is this your army, Alhazred?"

"Every Caesar must begin somewhere."

"They have never been outside this mountain. They will be terrified of the wind."

"Then they will have to get over their fear," I answered harshly. "I am a potter and they are my clay. I will fashion them into what I need to accomplish my purpose."

The men who had gone to fetch the weapons returned and piled them at the foot of the stairs. Even at a distance I could see they were much decayed. The leather windings had rotted from the hilts of the swords. The blades were pitted and green with verdigris, for the majority of them were bronze and not iron. Even the iron weapons were so rusted and decayed, not one in five would survive a single stroke in battle.

"It does not matter," I told the girl. "We will strike Jubbah in the dark of night, when all the inhabitants of the village lie sleeping. The ghouls will attack the Bedouin, and the Thamud will go into the houses and subdue the men before they wake."

"Do you intend to slaughter them all?"

I look at her in surprise. Did she really believe I would do such a thing?

"To the contrary, I will spare as many as I can. I need soldiers who can fight under the sun. The men of Jubbah I will send out to all parts of Arabia with the message that a great army is being assembled at the oasis. Mercenaries and even householders will flock to my banner once they realize the plunder that will be theirs. The ghoul clans I will unite together as my fighters of the night. They will spread terror of my name wherever they strike, and I will see to it that they strike far and wide."

"You have a grand vision," she said. "I liked the old Alhazred better."

"Put him from your mind. He is gone forever. He had a narrow soul with small dreams. I will not stop until all of the Caliphate is mine, and then I will turn my swords toward Byzantium."

"You sound half-crazed."

I studied her unhappy face. "You are alive because I know I can trust you and may have use for your services in the future. I feel no sentiment toward you. If you cease to serve me I will have you executed."

"That is plain enough," she said, a storm of anger brewing in her pale gray eyes. "How went your coupling with the witch last night?"

"My dealings with Salamagoogah are not your concern."

"What you speak about me behind my back you can say to my face," the witch said from the base of the stairs. I do not know how long she had stood there listening.

"It was nothing of importance," I told her.

She began to mount the steps, staring scornfully at Martala all the while. The girl did not flinch, but met her gaze. Some part of me admired her for it.

"I have come to inform you that your mercenary has returned with a force of ghouls."

"Excellent. How many are there?"

"I did not wait to count them."

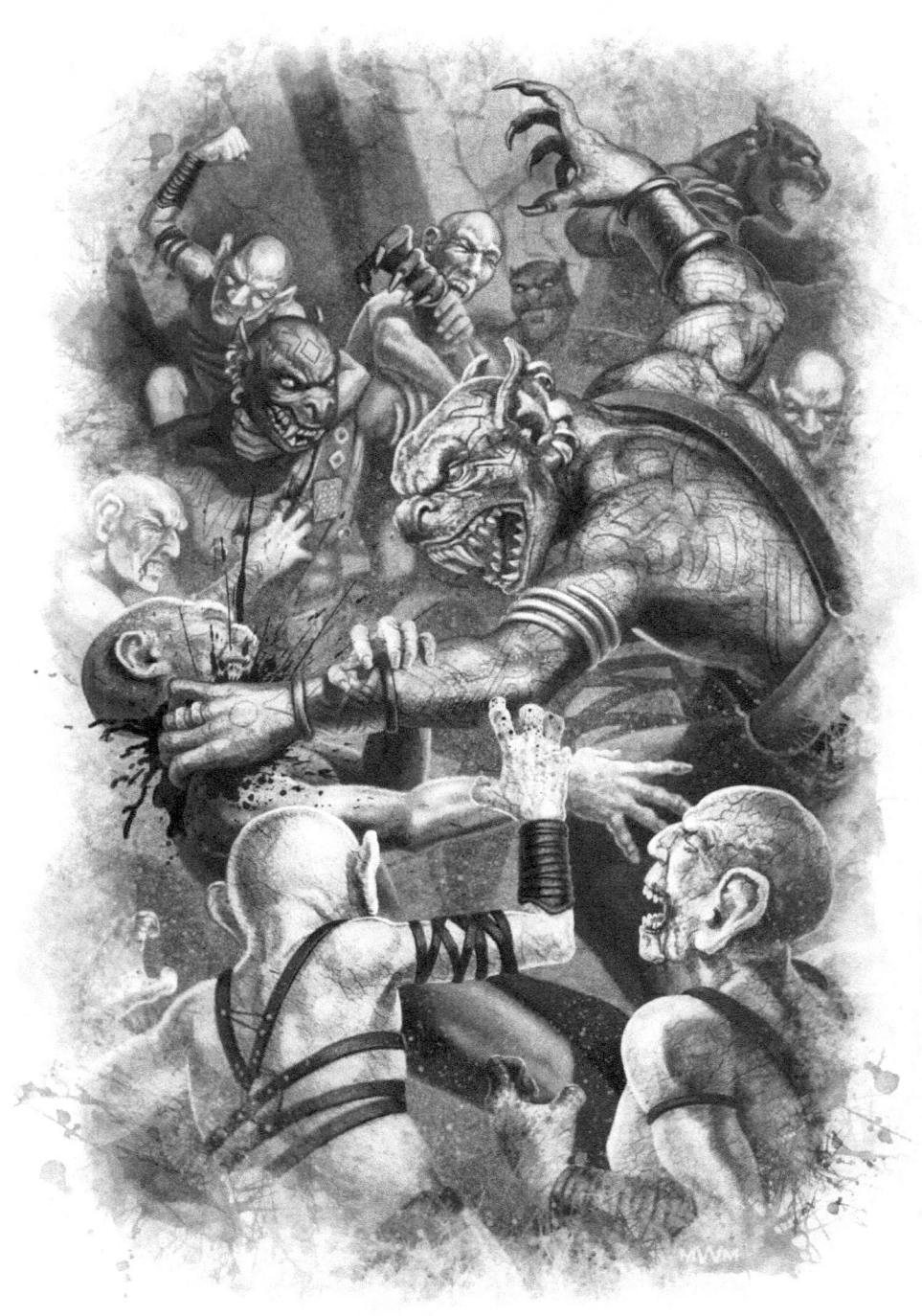

They fought with their teeth and fingernails ...

"Have them brought into the tomb chamber where I can look them over."

She called down in the Thamud language, and a slightly built gray creature scurried away with her order.

The ghouls entered in a double file with Altrus and Bakka at their head. I nodded at them with approval. They numbered eighty-four, and all of them were hunters and fighters. I could have wished for a greater number but these would serve for my immediate purpose.

"Welcome, Bakka of the Green Earth Clan," I said in the ghoul language. "You have answered my call. This will not be forgotten when the plunder is divided."

Bakka mounted several steps, regarding me strangely. He tilted his head like a puzzled dog.

"Are you still Alhazred of the Black Spring Clan?"

"I am Alexander," I told him, putting my hand on the surface of the red stone at my belt. "I am Caesar." My voice echoed from the dome above.

He came a little higher and sniffed the air.

"But are you still a ghoul?"

"What matter such trifles? I am greater than any ghoul or any man. I am a god."

Bakka turned to look down at Altrus.

"You were right."

He leapt at Salamagoogah with his black claws spread wide. She dodged his death strike with incredible swiftness, then turned and fled down the other side of the tomb. He scrambled to his feet and loped after her, yelping with bloodlust. Altrus drew his sword and bellowed a command in the Arab tongue, which the ghouls understand well enough. The ghouls gave forth a fierce cry in response and turned their claws and teeth upon the Thamud.

"Defend yourselves," I cried in the Thamud language. "We are betrayed."

The slaughter was sickening to watch, even for me. The Thamud did not even try to reach the pile of decayed weapons. They fought with their teeth and fingernails, but these were as nothing to the fangs and claws of the ghouls, who ripped out each throat with a single slash. All of the males were gathered in the tomb chamber at my order. Even though they outnumbered the ghouls by almost ten to one, they never had the least chance of victory. The ghouls took losses as well. The Thamud were able to overpower them at times by sheer force of numbers as they fought to the death in defense of their ancient home, and in defense of the red stone.

I called commands to the Thamud above the screams of battle but was unheard or unheeded. So great was the chaos that even with the authority of the stone possessing me it was impossible to restore order. Drawing my sword, I prepared to descend to the floor to fight with the Thamud against the traitorous ghouls, when I noticed Altrus mounting the steps, his sword in his hand. He wore a serious expression that I knew well.

"So you mean to kill me," I told him. "I was a fool to think I could trust you."

"The old Alhazred can trust me to the death, but you are not the man I knew."

"You want the red stone for yourself."

"No."

"You're lying. You won't get it. The stone makes me invulnerable."

"So you say."

We clashed midway up the stairs. I was much stronger and faster than I had been before I possessed the stone, but so great was the mercenary's skill with a sword, I was not able to beat down his blade. We fought for several minutes, which in a sword fight is equivalent to an aeon. I cut him on the arm and the thigh, but the flow of his blood only seemed to invigorate him. His sword touched me deeply in several places but I did not feel its sting and no blood flowed from my wounds, which closed themselves. I was gratified to see that my body did not tire. The stone renewed my vigor.

There was only one possible outcome to this battle. Or so

I thought. I did not notice the girl behind me as she threw herself at my legs and encircled them with her arms.

"Now, Altrus, strike now," she cried.

In that instant I felt a pang of regret at her betrayal. They had all betrayed me. Then my confidence reasserted itself as the warmth from the stone flowed through my body. What did it matter? I was a god. I would kill them all.

Chapter 23

is sword point slashed across my waist. I laughed at him.

"Are you trying to disembowel me? Don't you realize nothing you can do will harm me?"

Suddenly a great emptiness opened in my heart, as though a cistern had burst and all its pent-up waters were pouring forth into the sand. It staggered me and bent me over. I saw the stone roll and bounce down the steps, one after another. I could have leapt after it, but my strength had left with it along with my self-confidence.

I staggered and stumbled, and my sword slipped from my lax fingers. Altrus caught me against his shoulder. Instinctively, I hugged him as a terrified child hugs its father. I felt cold and alone, and so very empty. I saw my true self in that instant and knew I was a fraud. All my grand plans of conquest had come from the stone. None of it was my own will. I felt soiled and abused. It must be what a woman feels after she has been raped. I loathed myself.

Martala held me on one side and Altrus on the other. Without their support I would have fallen. Tears streamed down my cheeks. I could not speak, so great was my shame. We watched the remnants of the battle on the floor below. The ghouls had lost half of their number, but only a scattering of the Thamud remained alive, and they were being swiftly hunted and killed. So much for my great army of the night.

I raised my hand to my face. My nose was gone and my cheeks were scarred. I felt for my ear. Gone as well. There was no point in feeling between my thighs. I knew what I would fail to find there. When the stone dropped from my belt, it took my face and manhood with it.

You have returned to me, my love, Sashi said within my mind.

Her beautiful face floated before my tearful vision. I squeezed my eyes shut and blinked to clear them. I could not remember the last time I had wept.

Can you ever forgive me, Sashi?

There is nothing to forgive. You could not resist the power of the red stone.

I looked for it amid the creatures locked in combat on the floor but could not see where it had fallen.

"Where is Bakka? He needs to call off his ghouls or they will kill all the Thamud."

"He ran after the witch. They went down one of those passages," Altrus said.

I tried to call off the ghouls in their own tongue but they ignored me. They were insane with bloodlust.

"We need to find the stone and take it out of this place."

Martala stared at me with horror.

"Leave it where it lies. It's too dangerous."

A part of me yearned to pick it up and feel its vitalizing heat flow through my limbs.

"If we don't carry it away, the witch will regain control over it."

"Bakka will kill the witch," Altrus said with confidence.

Even as he spoke, I saw her emerge from one of the dark passages. She was naked. Her long, dark hair hung down her back almost to her waist, and her green eyes caught the glow from the lamps and seemed to flash with lambent fire. There was blood on her face around her mouth, and more blood covered her hands and forearms almost up to the elbows.

With an elegance of movement that was spellbinding to watch, she began to kill indiscriminately everything that came close to her. Ghoul or Thamud, it made no difference. Her hand lashed out, and the snap of bones sounded above the cries of strife. Or it caressed a neck, and the throat was torn out or the head torn off.

I wiped my eyes to clear them and peered around until I found my sword. Martala and Altrus stood watching the witch kill as though it were some kind of dance.

"Bakka is dead. Find the red stone. We must get it out of here."

To their credit, they did not argue but descended the steps and began to search among the dead and dying for the stone. Corpses littered the floor, which was slick with blood. I began to turn over the still-warm bodies, wary of a dying snap of teeth or slash of claws. No precaution was needed. Those who still clung to life did not have the strength to attack me. It leaked rapidly from their wounds to the stone beneath them.

The noise of the fighting had greatly diminished. I looked up to see Salamagoogah slay the last of the Thamud, a youth she picked up in one hand by the neck. Her fingers clenched and the sound of crushed bones was loud even over a distance of a dozen paces. She continued serenely toward the remaining several ghouls, who backed away from her with snarls on their snouts.

A dull red glow drew my gaze across the floor behind the witch. There was the stone, nestled beneath the corpse of a ghoul in the small of his back. It had rolled free of its leather sling. I hurried over to it while the witch was still occupied and turned the ghoul off it. Without even thinking I started to reach down toward it.

"Alhazred, no," Martala called behind me.

I realized my danger and drew my hand back just before my fingers brushed it. Here was a problem. How could we carry the stone when any sling or pouch would transfer its power to the carrier? Perhaps if it were carried far enough away from the body, this contact would not occur. I looked around for something with which to make a long sling, but the bodies of Thamud and ghouls alike were naked. Shrugging philosophically, I stripped my thawb over my head and stretched the garment out beside the stone.

"We will carry it the way Mohammed is said to have carried the black stone at Mecca, in a sling of cloth," I told the girl.

"How will we roll the stone onto the cloth?"

I looked around but saw nothing that looked long enough. I did not trust that the length of my sword blade would insulate me.

"Pick it up, Alhazred. It calls to you. Can't you hear it?"

Salamagoogah had finished her killing. She came gliding across the blood-drenched floor with her arms widespread, her bare feet floating on the air an inch above it. Altrus and the girl moved to bar her way with their weapons at the ready. As she glided nearer, she began to change in form. Her pale skin turned black and her extended arms transformed into leathern wings. Her body became squat and bat-like, and her bare feet curled into hooked talons. Claws replaced her hands on the tips of her wings. She grinned, and a thousand teeth as sharp as needles bristled forth.

"Strike at her claws and teeth," I told the others. "They must materialize to cause hurt. If they are solid, they can be injured."

Altrus went forward swinging his sword in a powerful two-handed stroke. The blade rang off one of the witch's talons as she raised her foot and drew back for a moment, but to our disappointment the blow caused no discernible damage. Even so, it must have given her some pain because she became more wary of his sword.

There was little the girl could do with her tiny dagger, but she struck and struck again whenever the witch drifted within her reach. The blade rebounded from her jaws and talons like a child's toy. It was evident to the three of us there could be only one outcome to this battle.

A fierce buffet from one of her wings knocked Altrus back. He tripped on the corpse of a Thamud and his foot slipped in a pool of blood. He fell backward across the corpse. The girl was too far away to guard him while he scrambled up. The witch darted in for a killing slash.

"This is what you want, witch," I yelled.

"Alhazred, no," Martala cried out in alarm as I bent to pick up the red stone.

The instant my fingers touched it, the most exquisite flood of pleasure and satisfaction flushed through my veins and made my heart double its beats. Once more I was a god, the ruler of the world. All my senses reeled with intoxication.

The witch paused to cackle at me, hovering above Altrus with her enormous black wings beating the air. Her inhuman face was twisted into an expression of triumph.

Without pausing my initial motion, I continued to lift the stone upward and threw it in an underhand cast directly at her head. This, she had not anticipated. Her wings cupped the air strongly as she threw herself backward, but it was not far enough or fast enough. The stone struck her in the chest and she reflexively curled her body to wrap herself around it.

The consequence was both immediate and horrifying. Her entire body burst into flames at the same moment and began to burn with furious intensity, as though fanned by a great wind. Her shrieks of agony rang in our ears. No human throat could have made such screams. When her wings burned away, her charred body dropped to the floor on its face and continued to burn until there was nothing left of it but glowing ashes. In their midst rested the red stone, undamaged by the fire.

Picking up my thawb, I carried it forward to lay it beside the embers.

"We must hold the stone in the center of its sling," I said. "Do not let your hands come closer than two cubits as we carry it. Martala, find a long shaft among the pile of weapons that we can use to roll the stone onto the cloth."

"No," Altrus said, his voice ringing forth in the stillness of the tomb chamber.

"What do you mean, no? Do you have a better way to carry it?"

He did not answer, but went to the pile of weapons. I thought he was looking for a pike or spear with which to roll the stone, but he drew from the pile a war hammer. With a grim expression on his face, he carried this back to where we stood.

"What are you doing with that?" I asked in growing alarm. On some level I sensed his intention, but my mind would not allow me to believe that anyone would do such a thing.

He did not pause, but swung up the hammer in both arms as he came forward, and brought its rusted iron head down on the red stone. The wooden shaft of the hammer snapped into two pieces from the force of the blow, but not before the stone cracked beneath it like a walnut, and fell into a dozen fragments. As it broke apart, the fragments of the stone lost their glow.

"What have you done?" I demanded in horror.

"What should have been done centuries ago," he said. "The world can survive without a god of war."

I hesitated to touch the fragments, but eventually steeled my resolve and brushed my fingers across the largest of them. I felt nothing. It was like any other bit of stone. Even its warmth had gone.

I straightened my back and looked around the tomb chamber. Apart from we three, there was nothing in it but death. Somewhere in one of the dark passages, I knew that Bakka lay in his own blood with his throat torn out, or perhaps with his back broken. There were female Thamud and young ones in the deeper tunnels. In time they might repopulate the mountain, but they would have nothing to guard. The red stone was no more.

Bending to pick up my thawb, I flicked it to shake off the ashes that clung to it and put it on, then found my belt and sheathed my sword in its scabbard. Altrus silently gave me back Gor's skull, and I tied it to the belt.

"The Caliph will not be pleased," Martala murmured.

"The Caliph can go hang himself," Altrus said.

I placed a hand on the shoulder of each of them, looking from one face to the other. For some reason I found myself smiling.

"There is nothing for us here. Let's go back to Damascus."

Chapter 24

he Caliph received me in the same study where we had last spoken together. He listened to my account of the events at Jubbah without emotion. I held back little of what happened, other than the restoration of my manhood, my sexual union with the witch, and the fact that Altrus had broken the stone. I told Moawiya that I had swung the hammer to shatter it. He was a shrewd man. How much he guessed of what I withheld from him is difficult to know, but his expression was skeptical when I said that I was the one who destroyed the red stone.

"I am surprised you could summon the power of will to do it, after being so completely overcome by its magic."

"Sometimes we surprise ourselves."

"Indeed." He stood up with restless nervous energy and paced back and forth across the floor in front of his desk, wringing his hands.

"So close," he muttered. "You came so close."

"The stone would have changed you. Are you really sure you would want to hold it, knowing what it would do to you?"

He stopped and stared at me for a long time.

"No, I am not sure," he said at last. "Upon reflection, it may be for the best that the stone was lost. I wanted it to use its power for good works, not to plunge the world into war. Foremost, I wanted to ensure that Marwan never got his hands on it."

"The black stone still exists at Mecca," I reminded him. "I know not what transformation it may confer on those who hold it, but it should be remembered that the Prophet prevented the leaders of the city from touching it when he had it moved to its present location in the Ka'bah."

He nodded seriously.

"I must think on this matter long and hard, but I will tell you now how my mind tends. It may be that the world would be a better place if the black stone were also broken into fragments, so that its power was stilled."

"Would it be possible to do such a thing? Many would be outraged."

"It would require statecraft and subterfuge. If it were ever to be done, no hint that I was responsible for it must ever become known. It would be better to fix the blame on a foreign power, or on a small group with revolutionary intentions. But I must give serious thought to this matter before I act."

"There is yet one more stone, the white stone that was said to unite the power of the red and black."

"That stone may remain safely hidden until the end of days," he said with a smile. "As long as no new information about it comes to light, no one can even attempt to look for it."

"Where do you suppose these three stones originated?"

"Legend says they fell to earth from heaven. It is my belief that they are not of this world, but come from the spaces between the stars."

"There may be more of them."

"It will be as Allah wills it," he said fatalistically. "From what you have told me, I now believe it is not right that men possess them."

"If you wish, I will go with my companions to Mecca and remove the black stone from the Ka'bah."

He laughed aloud, just as he had done the last time I made the suggestion.

"No, Alhazred. I do not doubt your ability, but if the black stone is to be shattered, it must be done in a way that appears to be the hand of fate."

He went to a cupboard and drew from it a small chest of dark wood that was reinforced at its corners with brass. Carrying this with some difficulty back to his desk, he opened it. I saw that it was heaped full of gold coins.

"A small payment for your service."

I bowed my head. "You are most generous."

"It is nothing, only gold. It will not buy loyalty, or trust, or friendship. It will not keep the assassins from my bedchamber or the treasonous whispers from my harem. They gather against me, Alhazred. I fear there may soon come a day when I am compelled to give up my throne."

"I am your friend. You have my loyalty, and you may trust me."

He smiled sadly and patted me on the arm. "I know. If only I had a thousand such as you, I would prevail, but my enemies are legion."

The audience was over. I hesitated.

"Yes? Is there something else you wish to say?"

"It is a trivial matter, but it would gratify me if you would grant me your indulgence."

"Name your purpose."

"I want you to send your royal guard to Jubbah to torture and execute the mayor of the town, a man named Hafiz ibd Ahmad."

He studied me with a pensive expression.

"I suppose you have a reason for this extraordinary request?"

"The mayor is corrupt and abuses his office. This I observed with my own eyes."

"Surely that is a matter for the town council of Jubbah to correct."

"They are undoubtedly just as corrupt as the mayor."

"What you ask is quite irregular."

"Will it help to decide you if I say that it is the wealth of Marwan ibn al-Hakam that has corrupted him?"

His face hardened. "It shall be done. What form of torture would you like?"

I pretended to consider the matter.

"In this instance, I believe red-hot pokers applied to the skin would be appropriate."

He called his guard and assigned a man to carry the casket of gold coins back to my house. I left him alone in his little room with his books, feeling a sadness in my own heart. Our destiny cannot be denied. Had I delivered the red stone to him, he would have conquered his enemies, but he would no longer have been the man I admired. In time the stone would have passed into the hands of one who was less wise and less compassionate. It was better that he should rule for a brief time and pass away. At least he would be remembered for his own good works. There was no place among men for a god of war.

When I returned to my house in Scholar's Lane, Altrus met me in my front hall. A woman I had not seen before stood beside him. She was about thirty years of age, with a serious but pleasant countenance. Her tall, slender body was modestly dressed and she wore few ornaments. Lustrous dark hair framed her face. Her eyebrows were thick and very black, but not unattractive. They framed her dark eyes. She looked Persian, or perhaps half-Persian.

"Alhazred, this is the woman I told you about," Altrus said. He was nervous, which was very uncharacteristic of him. "Her name is Nealayna."

She smiled and nodded.

"I wish to bring her into your house to live with me," he continued. "She was recently widowed. Her husband was a merchant with ships in the Lebanon. He was killed on the caravan road and his debtors have taken his house in payment of his debts. She has no place to live."

"You did not need to ask," I told him. The casket of gold coins made me cheerful and careless. "Certainly she may stay with you in this house."

"I thank you, Alhazred," she said solemnly.

"Are you not frightened to dwell in the house of a necromancer?" I asked her out of curiosity. Most citizens of Damascus would not even walk in the Lane of Scholars.

"Altrus has told me about you," she said. "No, I am not afraid."

I watched them climb the stairs together, wondering how in the world Altrus had come to know a cultured Persian widow. My joking remark about the patter of a little Altrus running through my house suddenly did not appear so absurd, or so amusing.

Martala returned after directing the Caliph's guard where to set the box of coins.

"What did you think of her?" she asked.

"Time reveals all things," I said cryptically.

"I like her. She's a Persian, you know."

"I did not notice."

"Altrus is in love with her."

"That is a complication I did not need in my life."

"It's Altrus's life, too," she said hotly. "The sun does not revolve around you alone."

Since I could not refute her truism, I merely shrugged and retired to my back garden to read the *Metamorphoses* of Ovid. Change was inevitable in life. I had learned that hard lesson in Yemen. I was prepared to be open-minded about this Persian, but as I have mentioned, I give my full trust to no one. Time reveals all things.

About the Artist

M. WAYNE MILLER is an illustrator for numerous book and magazine publishers as well as several role-playing game publishers. His list of clients includes Dark Renaissance Press, Tor/Forge, Dark Regions Press, Marietta Publishing, LORE Publishing, Thunderstorm Books, Genius Publishing, Journalstone Publishing, Gamewick Games, Dias Ex Machina, Chaosium, and Orson Scott Card's *Intergalactic Medicine Show*. Wayne continues his quest to learn and grow as an artist and illustrator. He lives in Greensboro, NC, with his wife, Carmen, and a very large cat.

About the Author

DONALD TYSON was born in Halifax, Nova Scotia. He writes a broad range of fiction and nonfiction based in the Western esoteric tradition. He is the author of the novel *Alhazred*, and the nonfiction works *Grimoire of the Necronomicon, The 13 Gates of the Necronomicon, Necronomicon: The Wanderings of Alhazred*, and the *Necronomicon Tarot*, all by Llewellyn. Most recently, his short novel *The Lovecraft Coven* was published by Hippocampus Press. He lives in Cape Breton, Nova Scotia, with his wife, Jenny, their American bulldog, Ares, and their Siamese cat, Hermes.

Colophon

The text was set in Clavo Book.
Caliph, Harquil, Matura MT
Script, and qurban feast were
used for titling; Mohammed
was used for drop caps.